BREVET RIDGE

Harry and Jack Ridge sought revenge on those responsible for killing their father and endangering their inheritance and livelihoods. In town, Lincoln Waittes and Gabriel Bonnet had contrived to form a conflict concerning Harry, Jack and the neighbouring ranchers. And along with an alliance to fabricate murder charges, they created a lynch mob. But some townsfolk had a surprise for the alliance. At last the Ridges had some help in their fight for fair dealing and their hard-won land.

ABE DANCER

BREVET RIDGE

Complete and Unabridged

LINFORD
Leicester

First published in Great Britain in 2007 by
Robert Hale Limited
London

First Linford Edition
published 2008
by arrangement with
Robert Hale Limited
London

British Library CIP Data

Dancer, Abe
    Brevet ridge.—Large print ed.—
    Linford western library
    1. Western stories
    2. Large type books
    I. Title
    823.9'2 [F]

    ISBN 978–1–84782–204–8

Published by
F. A. Thorpe (Publishing)
Anstey, Leicestershire

Set by Words & Graphics Ltd.
Anstey, Leicestershire
Printed and bound in Great Britain by
T. J. International Ltd., Padstow, Cornwall

This book is printed on acid-free paper

For the illustrator, friend and wife
Raphilena Margaret . . . love
and many thanks

1

Tobacco smoke drifted slowly though the warm air, loitered in soft curling clouds above the tables of the Cooncan House Saloon. The tang of stale beer and whiskey rose sweet and pungent from the sawdust and wood-chip that crusted the floor.

A curious, dreadful fascination gripped the customers, and they sheltered their glasses and cards as the three men at the bar confronted each other.

Harry Ridge stood very still, his left hand hanging close to the stock of his revolver. Through long fair hair, his grey eyes held on to the man facing him.

Jack Ridge was standing to one side of his brother and, like Harry, his hand was close to his gun. It was one of a pair of matched revolvers that were built for their father by a skilled

Cincinnati armourer.

Harry's voice pierced the charged atmosphere of the saloon. 'You made a big mistake in still wearin' one o' them wrist garters, Bream. They always come in pairs.' Harry tossed a blue and yellow-beaded decoration onto the bar. 'You must've dropped it when you were shootin' my father, you gutless scum.'

Hawker Bream stood very still for a moment, then made the despairing grab for his big Army Colt that he carried across the front of his stomach. He wasn't that slow, just too late.

'An' that was your second big mistake.' Harry Ridge's mouth hardly moved as he brought his gun hand up and fired.

Bream's eyes froze as the .44 bullet blew the middle of his chest apart. He shuddered, and a rill of crimson oozed across his lips as he pitched forward in a lifeless heap.

Harry took a deep breath and swept the amulet down into the damp sawdust. Under a table, someone moved his hand and Jack levered back the hammer of his revolver.

'I'll shoot the first man that moves, then out o' panic I'll probably shoot someone else. Most of you will die,' he threatened.

A floorboard creaked, and at the rear of the saloon, Gabriel Bonnet stepped into view. He was the proprietor with the frock coat and silk, stick-pinned cravat. He took in the Ridge brothers and the stunned faces of his customers. Then he walked over to Bream. 'Who's responsible for this?' He toe-rolled the body with his boot, then looked impassively at Harry.

'Yeah, it was me,' Harry confirmed. 'An' I'll find who else was involved an' give *them* the same chance I gave *him*. You can tell the sheriff that.'

A grin spread over the gambler's face. 'You know Gemson's real protective of his authority in Comeback. If there's any killin' to be done, he's the one likes to do it. In the light of anythin' differ-ent, he'll regard this as murder.'

Harry took several steps backward. 'He can regard this as anythin' he wants. But Bream drew first, an' everyone here saw it.' He turned to the cowboys and gamblers who sat fearful in the saloon. 'You're doin' very good. Keep still . . . move nothin'.'

Matched closely in height and features, the brothers backed through the door and swung into their saddles. They galloped up the main street, but nothing came at them, save a mongrel that snapped bad-temperedly at the horses' heels.

'No one's followin',' Harry said, as they passed the outlying clapboards of the cow town.

'They've got time,' Jack shouted back, 'an' they'll all be sayin' you murdered Bream.'

The brothers eased their horses to a trot, and Harry leaned and punched Jack in the leg. If he felt any grief at having just killed a man, he failed to show it. 'I was pleased to see you, kid. But why've you come back?'

'That's the point o' this place . . . no one ever does,' he said with a slim smile. 'An' I thought they taught officers not to panic. You ain't been cashiered, have you? What do they call it, *bobtailed*?'

Jack shook his head. 'No, I ain't been bobtailed,' he said. 'Pa wrote me about the trouble he was expectin'. He as good as bankrupted himself gettin' me to West Point. If I'd got here sooner, it might have made a difference.'

Harry pulled the brim of his hat down tight across his forehead. 'Yeah, maybe, Jack. But I doubt it. The old feller never told me he was writin' you.'

The two riders passed through a rock-strewn gully that led to their home at the Sunbird. Jack unsaddled his horse to chomp the bear grass, and Harry led his into the barn. He stared at the Ozarks that glittered in the dipping sun, then followed Jack to the ranch house.

A short, stocky figure greeted them, and Harry said, 'Stern, this is my brother, Jack. Jack, this is Onslow Stern. He's from Blytheville, north o' Memphis. He's worked with us for a while now, mostly been helpin' Seth an' Max.'

Stern looked tough, but he had a stove-up leg that Jack couldn't help noticing. With a direct look, Stern challenged the man who stood appraising him.

'Pleased to meet you, Onslow Stern,' Jack said, and offered his hand in friendship.

'Yeah, it's why I'm just called Stern,' Stern said in response to Jack's interested look.

Harry turned toward the house. He was looking for Seth Carlisle, the ageing gun-hand who, years past, had sought retirement and seclusion at the ranch. 'Seth should be around somewhere,' he said. 'He'll be pleased to see you, Jack.'

Jack put his hand on his brother's shoulder. 'Reckon you got some explainin' to do, Harry.'

Seth stepped from the veranda that

fronted the house. He nodded in quiet, genuine pleasure, then turned into the open doorway.

In the ranch house, the four men sat around a table, and Harry told Jack about their father's death.

'I was across the Mossbank lookin' for slicks. I heard gunshots an' saw a rider, but he took to the higher ground through the pines. I found Pa with his horse standin' over him. He'd got two rifle bullets in his back.'

The nerves at the back of Harry's neck twitched with emotion. 'I tried to go after whoever it was I'd seen, but lost his trail beyond the timberline. It was late when I came back, so Stern rode to tell the sheriff early next morning. You might know his help didn't amount to a hill o' beans. That's when I decided to bring in whoever shot him.'

Jack muttered something about the meaning of 'bring in', and Harry looked up sharply. He rose from the table, walked to the open doorway, and looked to the darkening sky. 'Seven or eight days ago, I went back and found somethin' the sheriff hadn't. It was that armband — one o' Bream's little Cheyenne ornaments.'

By Stern's look, Jack could see that he didn't fully understand. 'You know some o' the set up, I'll give it to you potted,' he started. 'We, the Ridge family, own the Sunbird Ranch, an' the Mossbank River runs along the eastern border o' the valley. About ten years ago, a man named Radford Cayne bought a tract o' land below the flats. But there's a five mile bluff that cuts off the river from the ranch. There wasn't enough top water for a herd, so he had to bore, bring up water from the sinks. Not long after, he changed the existin' brand to RC, his own initials. Straight off, we called it Raisin' Cayne. Funny, it sort o' stuck.'

Harry turned from the doorway, and continued with the story.

'It was soon after that, we began losin' cattle. It weren't that difficult for

Radford to change our Sunbird mark to his own initials.' As Harry spoke, he rolled his toe around in the dust, indicated how the lower part of S, could be contained in R. 'All he had to do was get himself one o' them Kansas brand burners. Less than a year later, Tayler Gemson was elected sheriff o' the county, an' Gabriel Bonnet opened the Cooncan House. There's nothin' much for a hundred miles, so's plenty opportunity to rook the town. It was a gold mine from the start. Shortly after this, Lincoln Waittes arrived, an' opened the bank. It was badly needed, and it was ranchers' money that made it a success, although most of 'em didn't care much for Waittes. Pa noticed that with the exception of Cayne's ranch, almost every acre of Deepwater County was heavily mortgaged. Cayne's is the only ranch inside five hundred square miles that makes money, in spite of everythin'. Dad helped out the smaller ranchers with our water, and that's what Waittes don't like.'

Stern sat and nodded. Jack remained seated and placed his revolver in front of him. He unhinged the frame and idly turned the cylinder. 'Waittes, Gemson, Bonnet an' Radford Cayne are a sort o' mutual society, an 'alliance'. They've crushed most o' the smaller cattlemen by foreclosin' and callin' in loans. But they're stymied as long as Sunbird controls the water.' He snapped up the barrel of his gun. 'They've tried to force us out by rustlin' the cattle. It's a strong group, an' they control everythin'. Eventually Pa got too hard-pressed, an' had to take on a promissory.'

Harry turned back towards the land beyond their ranch. He looked into the night towards Comeback, and spoke bitterly. 'They knew he'd pay back the money; they knew him too well: so they shot him.'

Stern had been listening intently to the brothers. He sniffed hard before he spoke. 'How was them murderin' your father any use? *You're* now the owners. I can understand the sheriff not chasin' after the man he'd hired to do the killin', but . . . '

Harry carried on. 'Yeah, the Sunbird is ours, but we ain't got much chance o' keepin' it. The loan's still there. It's a lot more than we can raise, an' they know it. They stole most o' the breed stock, an' you've probably seen there's less than fifty saleable head.'

Stern grinned and shuffled his feet awkwardly. '*I* could help you. I've got money, had it for some time. It could never buy what I need.' He looked at Harry sheepishly. 'It's a long story, but you don't have to go to the bank. How much you lookin' for?'

Jack and Seth looked at Stern in surprise, and Harry shook his head. 'Thanks Stern, but I hadn't reckoned on borrowin'. Jack was right. Bonnet's goin' to scheme to get me charged. The only witness I've got is my younger brother, an' I think he's got his doubts.'

Jack smiled thinly. 'No, Harry, I saw what happened, but it'll make no difference. Gabe Bonnet'll testify against you. An' I wouldn't be surprised if there's a warrant out for your arrest right now. Payin' off the loan, or anythin' else, won't make any difference.'

'So what's to do?' Stern asked.

Harry strolled outside. He sat on a wooden bench and called back through the door. 'I'll stay here, an' wait for Sheriff Gemson.'

Stern followed him out onto the veranda. He looked serious. 'From what you say, you'll have to sell up. So what's to stop me biddin' for the Sunbird?'

Seth spoke softly to Jack. 'That's more interestin'.'

Stern looked inside. 'I'm not much of a hand with guns, Seth, but I know me numbers . . . can read some. I'll raise any bid they make.' He bunched his large strong hands, and turned back to face the pen range.

Far off, a column of riders was outlined black against the night sky. Changes in landscape were part of Stern's watchful nature and he'd seen them. 'Visitors about a mile away,' he said.

'That'll be the sheriff. Guess I'll ride the owl-hoot for a spell,' Harry muttered grimly.

Jack put his hand on his brother's shoulder. 'I'm sorry, Harry. I don't blame you for killin' Bream. I just wish . . . ' His words hung in the air.

Harry returned a kindly grin. 'You just wish it was different. Stern, if you're serious about this land, you'll need a big gun. Seth will show you how to use it.' He grabbed a coat, and walked towards the back door. 'Don't worry about the sheriff, it's me he wants. An' he knows what I'll do if any harm comes to any o' you or this ranch.'

'Hanged for a sheep,' Jack mumbled.

The three of them watched Harry disappear into the barn. Within minutes, he was galloping north. Seth and Jack sat thoughtful on the steps, and Stern was inside, nervy with the keenness of revenge.

2

Tayler Gemson slid from his saddle, and Jack and Seth stepped back onto the veranda of the ranch house. The big man came up the steps, and extended his hand in greeting. 'Jack, I heard you was back from that fancy New York military college.'

Jack hesitated a moment before shaking Gemson's hand. 'Yeah, well, someone has to go there, Sheriff. Right now, I'm takin' furlough. But what brings you to Sunbird, so late?'

Gemson laughed. 'I reckon you know that, General. You was there when that brother o' yours murdered Hawker Bream.'

'That's a mighty provocative choice o' words,' Jack said slow and thoughtfully.

The sheriff ignored it. 'I know it weren't *you* did the shootin', General.

14

It's Harry, I've got an arrest warrant for. We trailed him here, and I'm not arguin' the case. Where is he?'

Jack shrugged. 'No idea. He left a while ago, but never said where he was goin'.'

'I hope you ain't hidin' him somewhere, General. That would be a serious meddlin' with the law.'

Jack looked straight at Gemson. 'If he was anywhere near, you'd find it a lot worse than *that*.'

Again, Gemson ignored Jack's provoking. 'Harry should have come to me when your father got shot. Goddamn it, there weren't a shred of evidence.'

'Harry showed the goddamn evidence to Hawker Bream,' Jack snapped back at Gemson. 'That's why he went for his gun. It was self-defence. As my brother rightly pointed out at the time, it was Bream's second mistake.'

Gemson was losing the initiative. He took off his hat and wiped a heavy arm across his forehead. He looked at Jack and appeared to relax a little. 'The town's growin' fast, Jack, an' needs a deputy. Job pays forty dollars a week with full board. You get a bullet allowance too. There's no future for you, stuck out here, an' you know it.'

'I ain't stuck out *anywhere*, Sheriff, an' there's no goddamn future in bein' deputy sheriff o' Comeback, either. But if you're makin' me an offer, I'll do it 'cause right now I need the money.' Jack turned his back on Gemson and looked at Seth. 'An' from now on, you're goin' to call me Deputy — Mr Ridge, even,' he advised.

Gemson was surprised. 'What makes you so sure o' that, General?'

'Because if you call me *General*, one more time, I'm likely to wrench your fat jaw off.'

Seth nodded approvingly.

The sheriff was aware of the financial troubles that afflicted the Sunbird ranch, and made a tactless blunder. 'There's a reward of five hundred dollars to bring your brother in,' he said.

Stern drew air through his teeth, and Seth grunted loudly in disgust.

But Jack gave no sign of his feelings. 'That's generous o' the town, or's that Gabe Bonnet's money?' he responded quickly. 'I can't promise to catch Harry, but as a lawman I'll be tryin'.'

'Hm,' Gemson mused. 'So goin' for the reward's nothin' to do with it, then?'

Less than ten minutes after the sheriff and posse had gone, Stern was irritated and confused. 'I already said, I'll give you that money. You don't have to go after Harry.'

Jack shook his head, sensing Stern's allegiance. 'I think it's best that it's me that does, Stern. But I'm actually not. I've got somethin' else in mind.' He whacked his hat against Stern's shoulder. 'I hope Gemson fell for that, as much as you obviously did.'

Jack walked over to the body of a grandfather clock beside the fireplace. He opened the long-case, drew out a big Martini-Henry rifle, and handed it to Stern. 'Use it the way Seth tells you to,' he advised.

Cool night air drifted into the ranch house. Jack shoved the door to and turned to Stern. 'Ride east. Harry's out there somewhere, an' he'll see you before you see him. Tell him what's goin' on . . . to make for the lakes. *Then* you can let Gemson know.'

★　★　★

Jack had waited for Harry to get south of the Osage River, then he rode the five miles to Comeback.

Opposite the Cooncan House was a telegraph agency where Jack sent a message to his company commander at West Point.

He led his horse to the hitching rail outside the sheriff's office. Gemson was working on a reward notice, and he sniffed favourably at his handiwork. 'It ain't goin' to capture his soul, but it's good enough.' he observed.

'Why'd you need a notice, if it's me

that's bringin' him in? I do know what he looks like,' Jack said drily.

Gemson laid the notice aside. He fumbled in the drawer of his desk and flipped a silver star to his new deputy. 'Your badge.'

Jack caught it and put it in his vest pocket. 'I'll wear it when I'm sworn in. What about Harry an' that reward notice?'

Gemson rose heavily from his desk. 'You'll be in charge *here*. Your brother's headed for the lakes, so the dodger's for someone else's benefit. Meantime, there's a little somethin' that needs my personal attention.' Gemson grinned haughtily at Jack, stopped just short of calling him, General.

A little before noon, Jack saw the sheriff leave town and head south. The sun was high, and there was little activity in and around the main street when he checked into the hotel where he'd been full-boarded.

Jack was forking a potato when he heard quiet laughter from the door. It was Radford Cayne, and his daughter Nancy. The Caynes saw Jack and walked towards him. It had been five years since he had last seen Nancy. She had gone to Cape Girardeau on the west bank of the Mississippi to live with her mother, and Jack hadn't heard of her since. She held out her hand and he took it nervously. From the smudge-faced tomboy he remembered, she had grown into fine-looking young lady. Her eyes were cool blue, and her hair was the colour of an autumn leaf.

'Welcome home, Jack. This is a pleasant coincidence.'

Yeah, most agreeable, he almost blurted. He coloured with surprise, then spoke to her father. But he couldn't take his eyes from Nancy, who was so attractive and confident. He pulled out another chair.

'You could join me.'

Cayne considered Jack's plate of food. 'No, you just finish what you already started, Jack. Perhaps we'll talk later,' he said and started to move away.

'I am pleased to hear you've taken up the sheriff's offer. We need young men like you. Just out of interest, will you be bringin' your brother back here, to Comeback?'

'It's a murder warrant that's been put out, so reckon I'm obliged. Now that I'm a law officer.'

'It's a shame you weren't that when it happened,' Nancy said a bit brusquely.

Hmm, spiky too, Jack thought. But before he could remark on it, Cayne was steering his daughter away.

Jack didn't understand Radford Cayne. He didn't sound like the character he was supposed to be, and it didn't appear to be in his manner. He understood Nancy, but then she had a brother that he didn't.

Jack spent the afternoon browsing through the sheriff's records. He examined the Wanted notices, imprinting his memory with names, faces, and reward monies.

An hour before dusk, he visited the saloon. It wasn't a pay day, and the bar wasn't crowded. A dishevelled character, goaded by a colleague turned and watched him. Jack recognized the man, he'd been looking at a likeness of him less than twenty minutes ago, and he nearly recalled the name. The man finished his drink and took two steps forward. He almost made contact and Jack reeled from his feral odour.

News carries fast, and there was no doubt, it was meant to be a rough test of Jack's status and character. As he considered a move, he wondered why Gemson hadn't done anything. The face would have been staring up at him from his desk. ARMED ROBBERY. ESCAPED CONVICT WANTED IN OMAHA — NEBRASKA, it had said, and the man was known as Cousin Burnish.

Jack drew his gun and nudged the long barrel gently into the man's stomach. 'I normally ain't one for interruptin' a man's drink, but this ain't exactly normal, Burnish. You just gone an' got yourself arrested.'

Burnish was too surprised to respond.

His mouth opened and he stared blankly. Jack saw Burnish's partner reach inside his coat and he swung the revolver towards the ground. He pulled the trigger and a bullet tore into the man's toes. The man was cursing and howling with pain, but Jack pressed his advantage with the gun barrel back in Burnish's vest.

He whispered close to the side of the wanted man's face. 'I know what you're thinkin', feller, but this is one o' them newfangled, single-action Colts,' he lied. 'You wouldn't have time.'

Jack turned to the few customers of the saloon. 'If any o' you good citizens got an overpowerin' need to help, go get a doctor. This one's goin' back up the Missouri.'

The noise of Jack's gun brought Gabriel Bonnet from his office. He stared in disbelief, and Jack nodded at him.

'Evenin', Mr Bonnet. We seem to be givin' your friends a real hard time at this bar.'

Bonnet saw one of his hired men

with a smashed, bloody foot, and another with a gun stuck deep in his belly. He managed to hold his feelings, but not as far as his office door that slammed behind him.

Jack relieved Burnish of his short-barrelled Colt, and nudged him into Main Street, towards the jail. He kicked Lambert Benk, the jailkeeper and town marshal, awake. 'Get me the cell keys. You got yourself a customer.'

Burnish cursed and Jack pushed him forward. 'Make yourself at home, Cousin. Looks like there's a pail, but I'm guessin' the county don't run to bathin' facilities.' As Benk locked the door, Jack turned away. 'This weren't ever personal, you understand. It's only the money I'm interested in,' he said.

The marshal then showed some interest. 'The sheriff ain't goin' to like this. It'll get him madder'n hornets, yes sir.'

'You worry about me, rather than Gemson. If this feller, Burnish gets out, you'll owe me the five hundred dollar reward,' Jack joshed, as he walked past Benk.

As Jack returned to the sheriff's office, Benk peered into the jail, replaced his chair on the sidewalk and spat into the dust. 'Someone's goin' to clip that boy's wings afore too long. Jus' see if they don't,' he said grumpily.

3

It was several days before the sheriff returned to Comeback. Cousin Burnish continued to sweat it out in the jail, cursing and roasting anyone within earshot. Wanting bail for the prisoner, Gabriel Bonnet was waiting to see Jack.

Jack grinned and shook his head. 'I ain't got that authority, an' you know it. Burnish is wanted for robbery and jailbreakin', not spittin' on the sidewalk. He stays put, at least until Gemson gets back.'

Bonnet accepted the problem. A circuit judge wouldn't fix bail for an escaped convict, and as long as the sheriff was away, the deputy held the cards. However, Bonnet employed Burnish to protect his interests in the saloon as well as his own personal safety, and the man wasn't earning his pay sitting in jail. 'Every night someone rides in with a price on his head,' he started his indignant bluster. 'It don't bother Gemson. He turns a blind eye, as long as they keep their noses clean. Why there's probably half a dozen in my place right now, an' most o' them are from out o' state.'

Gemson's wayward law provoked Jack. Perhaps it would do the same to Bonnet. Jack took off his hat and pitched it across the office. 'Hmm, is that so?' he responded with quick interest. 'Tell you what. Give me their names, an' I'll see 'em bunk in with Burnish. It would be one hell of a way o' boostin' this here deputy's compensation.'

When a frustrated and discomfited Gabriel Bonnet returned to the saloon, he snatched at a bottle of whiskey, and beckoned two men to his office. If the newly deputized Jack Ridge continued to act the honest lawman, the Coon-can's profits would soon be taking a plunge.

Back at the sheriff's office, Jack was

toying with the notices of several wanted men. He pushed one of them into his open vest, buckled on his gunbelt and went out. When he reached the saloon, he pushed back the swing doors and walked straight to the bar. 'Where's Mr Bonnet?' he asked the bartender.

The man was ladling up pickled eggs, and he nodded towards the closed door at the back. 'In his office.' But when Jack started for the door the bartender held up his hand. 'I'd wait till he comes out. Best way, Deputy.'

The man's voice carried an unmistakable warning, and Jack stopped. 'I'll wait then,' he said. 'What's a few minutes between us? Perhaps you could let him know I'd like a word.'

Taking an egg, he went outside and stood against the saloon wall. A cowboy came out and nodded, and Jack watched him lead his horse along Main Street to the livery stable.

Within a few minutes, another man followed. But he was unaware of Jack until he felt the revolver's muzzle thrust into the base of his spine.

'Judgin' by the Wanted poster I've got here, you've a rare likeness to Mr Lorenzo 'Pepperbox' Church. Right down to the . . . ' Jack let the words trail. He lifted the man's coat and gingerly felt around his vest for the twin, pepperbox pistols.

Church started to argue, but Jack closed him down with a chilly smile. 'We ain't goin' to make a ruckus,' he warned. 'This is just between you an' me. Get yourself down to the jail, an' tell the marshal there — his name's Lambert Benk — to put you in a cell. If you don't, I'll come after you, an' you really wouldn't want that.' It was the slow shake of Jack's head, the waning smile that sent compliant fear through Church.

Later, when Jack arrived at the jail, Church was penned up next to Cousin Burnish. Jack told Benk to take away their buckets if they spoke to each other. 'An' if they start crowin', throw it over 'em.'

'Pourin' piss over prisoners ain't what I'm used to.'

'Just do it. Look on it as job satisfaction.'

Later the same afternoon, Jack arrested another wanted man. It was the cowboy who'd led his horse to the livery stable. He hadn't recognized him at first, only later when he checked the notices. The man was a cattle rustler from Kansas, and he was jailed alongside his cohorts.

*　*　*

It was mid-evening before Gabriel Bonnet was missing his men. No one had seen them, and he was concerned. He had anticipated something going wrong, and guessed that Jack Ridge was there with it.

There was a light in the sheriff's office, and Bonnet saw Jack slumped at a desk. His eyes were closed and he held a few reward notices in his hand. Others were strewn across the floor.

Jack blinked as he looked up. 'The mountain to Mohammed eh?' he said, as the saloon owner came in.

Bonnet used his gambler's front to disguise his irritation, his impatience. 'I was told you wanted to see me.'

'I did, yeah.' Jack pushed the notices aside. 'It was to let you know it weren't fear or favour towards Burnish an' his friends.' He squinted hard across the office at Bonnet. 'Hardly seemed fair to arrest *him*, when most of his cronies were still livin' it up in your saloon. You visited the town pen recently?'

Bonnet smirked. 'Hah. You've let Burnish go. I knew you'd see it my way in the end, Ridge.'

Jack got up, stood square on to Bonnet. 'No, you misunderstand. They're *all* there now. Burnish, Church, an' that Kansas cow thief. Tucked up like hogs for market.'

Bonnet *had* misunderstood, and was startled at Jack's audacity. 'That could be one hell of a big mistake, Deputy,' he barked.

He stomped from the sheriff's office

and went straight for the jail. Benk hadn't the nerve to stop him, and the prisoners howled with anger. Bonnet took one hard look, slammed the jail door against the frightened marshal, and returned to confront Jack. He was almost on the run, his body trembling with rage.

'You meddlesome whelp, you've no jurisdiction over those men.'

Jack was unmoved. 'Well, they're all wanted somewhere, Mr Bonnet. The sheriff can sort out the whys and wheres. Meantime, the world can sleep soundly at least for tonight.'

Before dawn, news would reach the nearby ranches. Regardless of any jurisdiction nicety, Comeback's new deputy had jailed three infamous law breakers.

★   ★   ★

Sheriff Gemson rode back into town the next morning. 'What in goddamn almighty hell's name do you think you're doin'? he exploded, on seeing the prisoners. 'They're not wanted in our county. They've broke no law in this town. Turn 'em out, immediately.'

Jack had intentionally bent the law. But to innocent, law abiding townsfolk, outlaws were being released into their midst.

* * *

The Sunbird ranch was coming up for auction, and Jack made several trips out to see Seth and Stern. The Mossbank, and its water still belonged to the Ridge spread, but if the town's alliance became its new owners, they would have a stranglehold on the smaller ranchers.

Through the expert guidance of Seth, Onslow Stern was becoming accomplished with the Martini-Henry and its capability. There had been no word from Harry, but it didn't concern Jack. The deputy knew his brother was more than capable of looking out for himself.

★　★　★

It was a public auction, and on the day of the sale, two men climbed from a prospector's wagon. Looking purposeful, and carrying the big rifle, not many would have recognized Seth's partner as the lame, reclusive Onslow Stern. The main street was thronged with stock wagons and horses and two, wide-tracked Murphy wagons from Jefferson City.

Seth tied their wagon to the hitching rail in front of the hotel, and Stern picked up a money draft on a Memphis bank. To him, it was a worthy split, for genuine, unconditional friendship.

Jack found them out back of the hotel where the auction was to be held. He looked serious when he saw Seth with a Navy Colt tucked into his pants belt, but grinned when he saw Stern. 'You look like you mean business. I thought you might've changed your mind.'

'Naah,' Stern said, returning the grin.

'I wouldn't want to miss the surprises when I buy myself a ranch.'

They'd been standing at the rear of the hotel for a while, when Stern whispered, 'Harry's comin' into town. I told him to stay away, but he wants to see the sale's run legal. An' I figure he wants to see you, Jack.'

Tayler Gemson stepped onto a makeshift platform, and Lincoln Waittes stood close for any financial or legal jargon. Among the crowd, Jack saw Gabriel Bonnet with Cousin Burnish lurking in the background.

Gemson read out a description of the property. The request to bid got started, and a man at the back opened with the expected desultory offer. As Jack turned to look, the rudiments of a depressing tale whirled around inside his head. *He* was supposed to be heading for General of the Army, and *Harry* was supposed to be a cattle king, with livestock to rival the Chisum outfit. Instead, they were selling up to a crippled trail hand who didn't even own his own rifle.

Jack cursed himself back to the reality of the sale, watched disconsolately, as Lincoln Waittes and his alliance teased for a serious buyer. In due course, the banker gave Bonnet his signal for the shock bid. It was Stern, though, who raised the offer and before Radford Cayne stepped in. Both bids were unexpected, and Jack saw Waittes's startled expression. He looked to Cayne, but it was beyond that he momentarily glimpsed the figure of his brother. Jack cursed to himself. As long as he was deputy sheriff, Comeback was the last place he wanted to see Harry, and he hoped that Gemson and Stern hadn't noticed.

Jack switched his attention back to Lincoln Waittes. There was something wrong. Radford Cayne was bidding against Waittes *and* Bonnet. But just as it looked as though the ranch was going to Cayne, Stern levelled out, 'Six thousand.'

A buzz of surprise, incredulity, then approval came from a few people in the hotel. Most of them didn't know Stern, had never really had the opportunity. But they knew he was with the Ridge family, and because of the headwater, a co-operative owner of the ranch.

Waittes's face had taken on a sickly, defeated pallor. He'd prompted Bonnet to raise bids, but the saloon owner failed to react. It was clear the man couldn't move any higher, and as auctioneer, Sheriff Gemson had no option. The Sunbird ranch was knocked down to Onslow Stern.

At the courthouse, Stern tendered the money draft, and had the Sunbird deed recorded. Jack told Stern to follow on and, with Seth, led off a small cheerful crowd. Jack looked around cautiously, but Harry was nowhere to be seen.

On reaching the swing doors of the saloon, somebody staggered into Seth's path. It was Cousin Burnish, and he wasn't as drunk as he made out.

Jack stepped back and shook his head. 'I goddamn knew it,' he groaned.

Burnish was leering at Seth, but without warning he spun around and pushed his left hand into Jack's face. His right hand reached for the snub belt pistol he carried strapped around his chest. But before he drew the gun, Seth was levelling his Colt between the man's shoulder blades.

A twist in the sidewalk planking had momentarily put Jack off balance. He'd seen the pistol, and a heavy thumb drawing on the hammer. He was wondering about his next move, the time he had left when, from the other side of the street, two shots crashed out in quick succession.

Burnish lifted himself onto his toes as the first bullet tore into his chest. Then he snapped forward as the second took him at waist level, destroying his gun and his hand at the same time. His face was rapt with shock as he stared down at fingers that were mashed to his gun. With one hand he clawed out for Jack, then closed his eyes and fell to the street.

Clutching a rifle, Gemson came running from the hotel. He stopped short as he saw Burnish's lifeless form ahead of him, Jack Ridge getting to his feet and rubbing his shoulder. For a second or two, the sheriff couldn't understand what had happened. It wasn't what he was expecting. He looked round and saw Stern approaching from the courthouse, his big rifle still in its scabbard. Seth was unmoved, his Colt unused.

From across the street, Harry sat calmly on his horse. His revolver was pointing straight at Gemson. 'Who you got to do your killin' now, Sheriff?' he called out. There was no other sound, just Harry's voice and a madly barking dog. 'Next time, I'm comin' for you, you son-of-a-bitch. Go talk to Bonnet about a loser's streak.' Harry turned and looked at the small crowd of onlookers. 'There's an election not far off. You people should get smart.'

Harry gently spurred his horse and cantered up Main Street. He headed out of town, west, towards the foothills of the Ozarks.

One of the ranchers who'd suffered from the town alliance turned solemnly to his wife. 'I'm goin' for a drink with Mole Painter an' Lemmy. We got to talk about a new sheriff.'

4

The men who were walking resolutely toward the Cooncan House, held up when Gabriel Bonnet suddenly appeared. Cousin Burnish was lying dead in the street, and Gemson was staring bewildered at the body.

'Every time I come out here, there's dead meat in front o' me.' The saloon owner cursed loudly, looked hard at Jack then spoke sharply to Gemson. 'You'd better get Ridge to a safe place, Sheriff. Get him where there's a rock to crawl under, an' before my boys see this. The man's bad medicine.'

Stern was at the edge of his patience, felt he had enough all round collateral to make a stand. He swung the barrel end of his big rifle against the underside of Bonnet's jaw. He drove it hard against the bone and stared into the man's face. 'You're the one needs a safe place, mister. If I just had a whiff o' this bein' your work, I'd . . . '

Stern's emotional exchange trailed off, and Bonnet shook himself free. 'Think yourself somebody now, do you? I was talkin' to the sheriff, you jumped-up nobody.'

Seth Carlisle edged a shoulder into the fiery space between Bonnet and Stern. 'Stay out, friend,' he offered to Stern. 'He's ridin' you . . . just guessin' at how this happened.'

Then Jack reached out and gripped Stern's arm. 'Seth's right. He's no idea, unless o' course, he was sat watchin'.'

'Who you sayin's killed him, Ridge?' Bonnet asked Jack.

Gemson roused himself from his thoughts and interrupted. 'It was Harry Ridge.' For the sheriff, it suddenly didn't look that good. Possibly he saw something of himself in Cousin Burnish, seemed dazed by the killing at his feet. 'He was defendin' his brother. I guess he had to. An' this body's got to be moved.'

Jack stayed around until the coffin-maker had removed Burnish's body, then he met up with the men at the bar.

Mole Painter was fulsome, on the verge of excitement. 'What this county needs is a new sheriff, Jack, an' we been talkin' it over. Would *you* accept, if we nominated and supported you?'

Harry's words had clearly made them all think, and fast. If Painter and a few more of the ranchers were prepared to back him, it was an idea. But meantime, he was the incumbent deputy, knew that when Gemson had collected his thoughts, he'd be organizing a posse for Harry.

Jack nodded. 'If bein' supported an' nominated, can be turned into votes, then yeah, I'll stand. I don't want to waste both our times, Mole.'

The old rancher offered his hand to Jack. 'You won't be, son, you won't be. An' well done.'

When Lemmy Muspratt suggested one more round of drinks, the bartender looked doubtfully at Bonnet,

43

who was talking to Gemson and Radford Cayne's son, Harvey. The saloon owner nodded, told the barman to serve it on the house.

On the way back to the hotel, Seth looked uneasy. 'They'll fight nasty, Jack. We know there's four you'll be up against.'

Jack smiled kindly at his old friend. 'Yeah I know. They'll need more.'

As they entered the hotel, the sprung bell above the door jingled. One or two of the customers looked up, and Stern nudged Jack in the side. 'That's the Cayne girl,' he said in quiet appreciation. 'She's a nice-lookin' kid.'

After their meal, Radford Cayne spoke to Jack about the work of a sheriff. He introduced Stern and Seth to Nancy, then kept Jack talking for ten minutes. Jack wanted to speak to Nancy but when he went outside, Stern had already volunteered to take her home. Jack laughed quietly as Nancy and Stern climbed into the prospector's wagon. He watched as they swung round towards Raising Cayne, didn't notice the man who slipped out of the darkness into the Cooncan House.

Jack went back into the hotel, and nodded at Seth who appeared half asleep. His hat was tilted down on his forehead, but the look was deceptive. Now that Jack had agreed to stand as sheriff, Seth would be ever wakeful, extra cautious.

Jack sat and talked events with Radford Cayne, then later, he met several other ranchers, and they discussed the likelihood of Stern withdrawing the water rights. They sat outside and, although it was dark, there was enough moonlight for Jack to make out the figure of Lincoln Waittes entering the bank. A few minutes later, Bonnet and Gemson followed. The alliance had decided to call a short-notice meeting, and Jack was tempted to listen in. He told the concerned ranchers that Stern would protect the Mossbank water deal, not renege on it. Then he said that he ought to be tending his regular night patrol.

He wandered off towards the sheriff's office, then doubled back to approach the bank in the off-street darkness. He pulled off his boots and climbed to the roof. Treading carefully, he reached a skylight directly over Waittes's office, through the dust of which he could just make out figures of three men. Within moments there was a sharp rap from below him, and Jack instinctively shrank back. He saw Gemson get up and open the door to let Harvey Cayne swagger in. The man was obviously drunk and he belched loudly, as he sat at Waittes's table. The voices were blurred, and Jack could only catch a word here and there, but he sensed they were talking about him. He gave a dry smile, thought something about those that listen at keyholes.

'An' how about that other little matter?' he heard Gabriel Bonnet say.

The banker nodded foxily. 'Ah, our little clod buster. I'm dealin' with it. I'll let you all know when I hear somethin'.'

A short, heated argument followed,

in which Harvey Cayne appeared to join in. It was some sort of problem, but after a while, they all got up and left the office. Jack lay still for a few minutes, then made his way down. He grabbed at his boots, and walked thoughtfully towards the sheriff's office. Now he knew. Radford Cayne wasn't connected with the men who were putting the squeeze on the town, it was Harvey. Any increase in the Raising Cayne stock was probably more to do with breeding than rustling.

Out of the darkness, an unsteady voice called his name. He stopped and waited as the man weaved a path towards him. The glow from a street side window lit up the side of the man's face, and Jack wasn't surprised by who he was confronted with.

'Harvey. Are you out lookin' for me?' Jack asked, as relaxed as he could.

Cayne stopped in the street, a few feet from Jack. He moved his feet around to give himself more stability. One of his feet seemed more wayward than the other as he tried to find stability. He grinned. Overall, it was the classic stance of a drunk seeking trouble.

'Yeah. Stay away from Nancy . . . my sister. An' stay away from me, too . . . everyone. But you will be . . . 'cause from tomorrow . . . '

Jack was suddenly bothered about what Harvey was trying to tell him. 'What are you sayin', Harvey? What *about* tomorrow?'

Cayne seemed to realize that he'd said too much. 'Why don't you try me now, eh Jack?' he slurred. 'You ain't got no help hidey-sneakin' in one o' these alleyways, have you?'

Jack stared down at Cayne. For many a year there'd been hostility. They'd grown up with it. They were roughly the same age, but as youngsters, Harvey had always been bigger, and had the muscle that went with it. It was Harry who had often rescued Jack after a raw beating.

The street was dark and deserted,

and Jack looked around him as he stepped off the sidewalk. Cayne smirked and started to undo his gunbelt, a deception for what he did next. Before the belt dropped, his right hand swung up. He was aiming for the middle of Jack's face, but Jack sensed it, and side-stepped with a fast punch. It was vicious, and cracked hard into Cayne's nose. Bright, thin blood spurted, and Cayne's face closed in on Jack as he attempted to focus. He wanted something to hit back at. But it was senseless coming in again, and Jack stood his ground at the reckless swing. He dodged the fist and stepped inside, made a hard, low stab into the side of Cayne's head. Cayne fell to his knees, snorking as Jack stood over him. He unwound himself into a crouch while Jack took his time, aiming with the tip of his boot. It was getting late and the best of the day was past for Harvey Cayne. The fray ended as suddenly as it begun, with Cayne being in no state to take any more.

Jack wiped his hands across the front

of his vest. 'You always did have more muscle than me, Harvey. Shame most of it was in your head,' he said, as he lumped Cayne across to the jail.

Lambert Benk was snoring peacefully on a cot, and Jack knee'd him in the side. 'It's me again, Benk. Get the keys. There's a drunk here, got himself into some trouble. Turn him loose when he sobers up.'

The marshal looked at the battered face, then at Jack. 'Who's that I'm seein' under all that snot an' blood? That young Cayne?'

'Yeah. It's a good job I'm turnin' in my deputy's badge. I could charge him with resistin' arrest or somethin'.'

Benk carried his usual burdensome expression. 'You're really tuggin' on Gemson's rope. Them two got a curious kinship. Closer'n a snake's belly to sand, some say.'

'There's always some as see the shameful side,' Jack retorted. But he was tired, losing his facility to care. 'OK, do what you like with him. It's late and I'm goin' to the hotel.'

The marshal lost no time in trying to bring Cayne round. He drenched him with tepid water, then dabbed at his bloody face with a bandanna. He tipped some coffee through his broken lips and then walked him around the cell. He found Cayne's horse and brought it round to the rear of the jail. He was interested to hear what had happened, but Cayne wasn't in the mood. He scowled, and told Benk to get out of his way. In the street, Benk slapped at the youngster's horse, watched it canter off to Raising Cayne.

★   ★   ★

Two miles out of town, Harvey Cayne met Onslow Stern in the prospector's wagon. It was heading east to the Sunbird ranch.

'I just been to your place,' Stern shouted, in a not unfriendly manner. Then as he got close, he saw Cayne's face, pasty white, puffed and sweaty in the moonlight. 'What the Sam Hill happened to you? Run into a some-time friend?'

Cayne pulled up his horse, angrily kicked it around a full circle. 'My face'll be mended in a couple o' days, gimp. Think on that,' he snarled thickly. But his meaningful look at Stern's busted leg changed when he saw the Martini-Henry, and he decided to leave any further insult.

Stern shrugged and flicked the reins. 'Must've been our Jack settlin' into his law work,' he chortled.

As Cayne pounded off in the direction of his father's ranch, Stern spoke to his wagon mule. 'No. With all the trouble that's brewin', I really ain't got time for more commitment. Miss Nancy's goin' to feel real hurt, but it's for the best, an' she'll have to get used to it. Perhaps Jack can help her through the pain.' He kicked the footboard and called into the night. 'Let's make for home.'

5

On his way back to the hotel, Jack called in at the sheriff's office. There was a lamp still lit, but Gemson wasn't there. He sat at the desk and thoughtfully penned his resignation. It hadn't been much of a term, and he wasn't overstaying his welcome, he thought wryly. But the way it stood, he'd had enough of being a deputy. Several times he glanced at the clock, guessed the sheriff was drowning some recent trouble.

Harvey Cayne's words had given Jack something to think about. There was no doubt in his mind they'd tried to kill him once already, with Cousin Burnish. And no doubt they'd try again. But it would be different next time. It wouldn't be a confrontation in the street or anything near to it. It would be something voiceless, probably out of the night. He thought back to the snatch of conversation he'd overheard at the bank, pondered on what the 'little cloud buster' that Waittes was waiting on, meant.

Harvey Cayne didn't strike Jack as a killer. Nevertheless, there were two bullets in the old man, and long distance with a rifle required the minimum of courage. And how much did Radford Cayne know about his own son?

It was getting late, but Jack's mind wandered on. He couldn't understand how any profit from the Cayne property helped the alliance. And with the exception of Raising Cayne, Lincoln Waittes's interest was credit allowance on nearly every ranch in the county. What Sheriff Gemson stood to gain was less obvious, although with Waittes's financial muscle, he'd have powerful support. Gabriel Bonnet's profit would come from an ever-spreading gambling empire.

Then another thought came to him.

What would they do about Stern? Try and destroy him? That wouldn't get them the Sunbird ranch, or water rights of the Mossbank. Besides, it would probably raise the interest of a more eminent state lawman.

Deciding it was useless to wait for the sheriff, Jack locked the door and walked to the hotel. But this time he was more watchful, did notice someone moving in the shadows.

In his room, Jack calmly lit a lamp. Then he pushed up the window, left a gap of a few inches and pulled down the roller blind. He took his pillow and pressed it roughly into the shape of a man's upper body and placed it on the bed. Then he covered it loosely it with a rucked-up blanket and put his hat on the bedside chair. He curled his belt around his holster and placed it on the pillow, close to where his head should have been, untidily spread a few of the other clothes across the floor, turned out the lamp and pulled the blind back open. Standing back from the moonlight that filtered into the room, Jack peered into the alleys that fronted Main Street. But he saw nothing moving, just heard muffled noise from the Cooncan House.

After nearly an hour of eye-aching surveillance, he drew a blanket around his shoulders and crouched in the corner of his room, to one side of the window. In the moonlight, he'd effected a convincing silhouette of a man sleeping.

Jack snoozed for another hour, then twitched alert at the sound of a scrape along the window ledge. The moon was lower, and from the windows, the shape on the bed was clearly outlined. He gripped the revolver that he'd tucked into his pants top and held very still. A hand appeared flat across the ledge, then another that eased gently upwards against the bottom edge of the window frame. As the window was slowly raised, Jack saw the head and shoulders of a dark figure. He waited for the optimum moment then he moved. He unwound from his crouched position and sprang forward. His arms were outstretched, his fingers grasping for the intruder's wrists. With both his hands, Jack gripped, put one foot up against the wall beneath the window and hauled back quickly and powerfully. For the merest moment, thin light outlined long hair drooping from a battered range hat. As the man's feet hit the floor, Jack drew his gun and slammed the frame hard into the back of the would-be assailant's head. He watched breathless as the man spread full length across the floor, then he kicked the hat aside and quickly reached up for his belt to wrap around the man's booted ankles. He glanced across the street, dragged the man up and out through the window gap, over the wooden sill and let go.

'Jeeesus, that'll kill him, if he ain't already,' he muttered, as the body thudded dully into the hard-packed dirt below.

Jack dropped to the ground a few

moments later. He heard the soft snuffle of a horse from somewhere across the street and he half dragged, half carried the man towards the sound. Jack assumed, hoped, it was the man's horse, as he pushed the body up behind the saddle. As he headed the horse out to Sunbird, one of many things turned over in his mind. What would have happened if he'd pulled the blind down and locked the window? He'd've come round to the door an' knocked, probably, Jack surmised and smirked grimly to himself.

The animal was a ripper and it struck a good pace. They crossed the dry bed of the Mossbank, and dipped towards the ranch house. Across the yard, he drew rein and yelled for some attention.

'What time do you call this? Whose horse is that, an' who's *he*?' Stern asked peering through the thin moonlight. He was wearing a long nightshirt and brandishing Seth Carlisle's Navy Colt.

'It's the goddamn Jack-O'-Lantern. What the hell are *you wearin*?' Jack retorted. 'Help me get him down, will you?'

Seth watched from a side window as Jack and Stern dragged the body into the house.

Stern stared at the man on the floor, then looked inquisitively at Jack. 'I saw Harvey Cayne not long ago. It was dark, but it looked to me like someone had a disagreement with his face.' He turned back to the man who was trying to raise himself onto an elbow. 'Could've been the same feller who did this.'

Jack stepped up close. 'Well, this one was of a similar mind to young Cayne.'

The man on the floor dragged himself to a half-crouch, grimaced with pain before speaking to Jack's boots. 'What the hell's goin' on?' he demanded.

Jack didn't answer, just stared down.

Stern knelt close to the man. 'Best tell us who you are, mister,' he threatened.

The man kept his mouth closed. He was trying to figure things out. He looked up at Jack. 'Who are you?' he asked through the hurt of cracked bones.

'The deputy o' Comeback, Jack Ridge. Now if you don't want any more pain just yet, tell me who it was paid you to break into my bedroom, back there in town. We both know you didn't come to tell me you hoped the bed bugs don't bite.'

The man looked insolently at Stern, then Seth.

Jack leant down and untied his belt from around the man's boots. Then without warning he pressed his heel into the man's chest. The man gasped, and his eyes blazed with pain.

'Huh, a few broken ribs,' Jack said. 'Now, tell me who it was who paid you to kill me.'

The man's chest was on fire and his breathing was laboured. He spat at Jack's feet and tried to raise himself further.

Jack guessed the man was already in too much agony to care about the threat of more. 'You've some hard bark,' he said. 'But a search party's goin' to be here soon, courtesy o' Gemson an' Bonnet. I've just hurt you some. They'll have you *shot*.'

The man scowled and swayed sideways. He wasn't fully understanding the corner he was in. 'You say you're the deputy sheriff?' he hissed. He had a thought process moving, but that was as far as it got.

Jack smiled almost admiringly at the man. 'Goodbye, mister,' he said. 'Stern, tie his hands again, then take him to the barn. Killin' lawmen *is* a hangin' offence.'

Seth turned and walked up to Stern. 'Let me give you a hand there,' he offered with a wink in Jack's direction. 'You might trip on your bloomers.'

The man still seemed indifferent to his fate, as Seth prodded him outside. Stern held an oil lamp and the three of them walked to the barn. Seth stopped and took down a coiled length of rope that hung from a peg outside the barn door. Then he looked hard at the man.

'Sometimes Jack Ridge gets very angry. Usually them times when he thinks of his pa gettin' shot. Then again, when people try to do the same to him. Yessir, *real angry.*' Seth kicked hard at the man's feet, watched grimly as he collapsed heavily into the open corn crib.

Stern wedged a stave across the long topflap, and banged it tight with his fist. 'An' keep quiet, or we'll come back an' use the rope.'

Jack told Stern he'd be using the long chair for a couple of hours. 'There's some faces I want to see in the mornin', just after they've seen mine. All the better since they won't be findin' that cove you ain't hanged yet.' He looked coyly at the new owner of his ranch. 'How'd you make out with Nancy?'

Stern smiled at the rib. 'I move too fast for her. Already, I'm way out of her reach. Other than that, we're a couple o' love-struck sidewinders. By the way, Jack, what was it you said you overheard Waittes sayin'?'

Jack shrugged. 'Maybe somethin, maybe nothin'. I think he was waitin' for some sort o' news.'

'Why not talk to Lemmy Muspratt? He hears things that are meant for others. Got ears in high places, apparently. Anyways, I hope somethin' happens soon around here that involves *me*.'

'It's a certainty, Onslow. An' *that's* a lot better than hope.'

★ ★ ★

In the Cooncan House Saloon, Gemson and Bonnet were opening another bottle. They'd been brought helpful news, were celebrating the demise of the deputy sheriff.

Gabriel Bonnet didn't give orders then casually expect them to be carried out. He believed there was no arrest for the wary, sent out men to watch other men. His watcher had remained out of sight, further down the alleyway, until he'd heard the hoofs of the other man's horse. He took the same route up the front of the hotel, and looked into Jack Ridge's small room. He saw the unmoving shape of a likely body, was fooled by the darkness. 'I saw your man Ridge. Looked like a big ol' hump rib,' he'd told Bonnet.

'Reckon we're lookin' to your re-election, Sheriff.' Bonnet poured himself another glass of French wine, and Gemson looked smug.

Bonnet looked favourably at his glass. 'How we goin' to handle Waittes?'

Gemson was a little confused. 'We got Ridge taken care of, didn't we?'

'Yes, Sheriff,' Bonnet agreed. 'I just wanted to hear you say somethin o' the sort. Like reaffirmin' an oath.'

★　★　★

In the meantime Jack had left Sunbird. At four in the morning he had no difficulty in reaching the town unseen. He left the horse in the alley where he'd found it, climbed back through the

64

window to his room and cleared the bed. He lay there staring at the ceiling, killing time for the first signs of light.

Somewhat unsteady from an excess of Bonnet's fine wine, the sheriff walked into his office. It was late in the morning but Jack was in the wash-house, waiting. The sheriff slumped at his desk, and the first thing that caught his eye was Jack's resignation letter. The content struck him funny. 'Yeah, resigned from life,' he sniggered.

'Got a joke to share, Gemson?' Jack's voice made the sheriff roll in his chair. Gemson's eyes bulged and it took him a while to focus properly. He suddenly wanted the can, but his legs refused to move. His hands started to tremble, and fresh sweat glistened across his forehead.

'I recommend a good night's sleep, Sheriff. You look like you can do with it,' Jack said.

The sheriff's expression made it certain. He'd been told that Jack was dead. Now Jack was back from it.

Gemson raised his eyes, sensed the direct vulnerability of his life.

Jack took a step towards him and the sheriff recoiled. Jack curled his fingers around the butt of his gun, and Gemson's face turned more sickly as he found his voice. 'What do you want?' he croaked, saliva flecking the corners of his mouth.

Jack laughed, but his face was grim. 'I just said it. Share the joke.'

The sheriff looked bewildered, and his mood became crafty. 'I was laughin' at your resignation here. That's what we been celebratin'. Don't surprise you, does it?'

'Well, yeah, it does a bit, Gemson. You didn't know about my resignation until a couple o' minutes ago. What you been celebratin' is me bein' *dead*.' Jack panicked the sheriff by moving nearer to the desk. 'Hah, I'm not goin' to kill you, Sheriff. Heaven knows it's mighty temptin' though. I want you to think on this. Cousin Burnish didn't die in the street as everyone supposed. He died in his coffin. He weren't exactly buried alive, but he weren't that cold neither. An' he did have an interestin' tale to tell before he stopped breathin'.'

Gemson's face sagged, and he looked as though his mind had wandered to a far off place.

Jack pushed his face in close. 'You need a lot to get out o' this one, you son-of-a-bitch. It weren't Burnish's confession, but it was just as good. Circuit judge should be makin' sense of it by now.'

The sheriff took a deep breath and a little courage seemed to return as he got to his feet, blustering.

Jack quickly drew Gemson's gun from its holster and stuck it to the big man's belly. 'Steady. Somethin' happenin' to me would be the fastest way to get a US marshal from Springfield or Jefferson City. I got friends an' family who'd see to that.' He turned the Colt in his hand and placed it on the desk. 'So you won't be needin' this, will you, *General*?'

Gemson sat down again. He couldn't think what Burnish might have said, but he knew that someone like him would frequently be condemned by what they knew.

★ ★ ★

For a long time after Jack had gone, Gemson thought about what had been said. Eventually, he realized it needed a more appropriate head than his, and he almost ran to the banker's office. Lincoln Waittes was no killer gunman, but he was the most ruthless of the group. The man was unscrupulous, his world was one of corruption and deceit. He had Gabriel Bonnet priced as second-rate, Tayler Gemson as a fool of limited use, and Harvey Cayne as a tiresome, risky young drunk.

Waittes had to make plans and, after hearing the sheriff out, he set up a meeting of the alliance for early afternoon.

6

Jack gave up his role as deputy sheriff, and returned to Sunbird. Except for the occasional loss of a heifer, it had been a sound year on the ranch. But it wasn't the same for the smaller ranchers to the south and east. Stern allowed their cattle to graze and water on his newly acquired land, but Lincoln Waittes had pressed hard. Every further loan he'd settled, had a catch clause, something slyly calculated to wipe them out.

Unnoticed by the sheriff, Harry came back to help out. Together with Jack and Stern, they rode the Breaks figuring out a way to defeat their opponents. They were surprised at Stern's horsemanship, and how he'd taken up the gun.

They were leading their horses through the foothills when Stern suddenly stopped. He pulled the

Martini-Henry from its scabbard and sat himself loose in the saddle. He levered a round into the chamber and looked hard ahead.

Guessing it wouldn't be the conventional way, Jack wondered how Stern was going to fire the big rifle, and he was right. Stern held the stock tight to his bad leg, and pulled the trigger. He levered shells in and out of the gun faster than the brothers thought possible. Stern pounded bullets into the low branches of a dogwood, and leaves and berries flew in all directions.

'Probably took a hundred years to grow, that did,' Harry muttered, as parts of the tree flew across the canyon floor thirty yards ahead.

Stern grinned excitedly. 'Yeah, well, no one's likely to come here for another hundred, so's plenty o' time to grow some more,' he exhorted. 'Seth showed me how to do that. An' if you think that was good, you should see him.'

'I can imagine,' Jack said calmly.

When they reached the grazing

ground, back near Sunbird, Stern turned to the brothers. 'I'm still learnin' about cattle, but it seems we could do with some upgrade stock,' he said.

Harry looked surprised. 'Yeah, you're right, we could. Why not go to the bank an' speak to Waittes? He should know the market, if anyone does.'

The following day, Stern did go to see Waittes. And the banker was obliging, said he knew of good stock for sale near the border country.

Within a few days the men rode out to inspect the herd. They couldn't find anything wrong with the animals or the sale. Brands had been run over 500 cross-bred shorthorns, but that was usual with border mavericks. Without further ado, Jack hired a drover to help with the drive, and they headed back home.

There was no sign of trouble until the cattle were in the dry lower reaches of the Mossbank. They'd camped for the night near the outlying borders of the ranch, and come daybreak, the drover was missing.

'That's real peculiar,' Stern said. 'You'd'a thought he'd want to draw *some* pay.'

'Yeah. I think we should worry about it a bit,' Harry said. 'Everythin's been a bit too sweet, so far. But we can handle the drive on our own from now on. Let's move 'em out.'

Once the herd was up and moving, Jack went ahead. They rode arrow outside the cattle, and Harry and Stern took turns dropping back to pick up strays. The ground was packed hard, but the surface clouded thick around them. They drew bandannas tight around their faces, and rode unseen.

They heard the Martini-Henry when its crash rebounded across the low foothills. Harry came at the gallop, and Jack swung wide from point.

'There ain't no goddamn dogwoods out there,' Harry yelled.

They found Stern crowding a group of cattle drovers. One of them was clutching his lower leg trying to staunch the flow of blood. Stern turned to face

Jack and Harry.

'These fellers believe our herd's mostly stolen. This one was goin' to use his rifle to help get 'em back. I gave him the ol' flesh notch. He's lucky . . . could've lost his leg an' half the side of his horse.'

Harry looked across the group. 'So, who are you men?'

'I'm ramrod o' the Hangin' Gate. An' it's our brand on most o' them cows,' a man in a dusty, home-spun brown suit said.

Harry looked over the herd and nodded. 'Well, I guess, that's a possibility, mister. But there's two things you got to bear in mind. One, we got a bill o' sale, an' two, you should see what Mr Stern's gun does from up close.'

The ramrod removed his hat and ran his hand across his plastered-down hair, considered the sweat on his fingers. 'Every ranch in the county's losin' stock, an' most of 'em are driven straight to the border where you picked those up. So a bill o' sale don't matter to me.'

'Well it matters to us, so this blue sky jabber ain't goin' to get us far,' Harry said, almost friendly like. 'We paid a good price for the cattle, an' we're not handin' them over to you, or anyone else. Why don't you just ride on? We're out of the Sunbird ranch, if anyone wants to take it further.'

The ramrod looked hard at the brothers. He saw the stone resolve and wasn't going up against it. He pulled up his horse's head and looked at Harry. 'Chance we'll meet up there, then. I know who you are.'

Harry shook his head and smiled. 'Yeah, I just bet you do. Probably did before you even got your horse saddled.'

As the men from the Hanging Gate rode off, Jack turned to Stern. 'Yeah, that'll be it. After you'd seen Waittes, he organized a make-up herd on the border. They all knew *I'd* be helpin' to run 'em back. Sidin' with a herd o' recently stolen cross-bred shorthorns, wouldn't do much for my nomination prospects.'

Harry smiled and looked at Stern. 'Whatever happens, you had the use of a drover for nothin', boss. You'll make Wall Street, one day.'

Stern went thoughtful. 'These cattle were bought out o' state, an' we paid honest money for 'em. Sure you pick up bad steers in a bunch, but it ain't goin' to stack too high as anyone's defence.'

The sun was a low, golden shimmer when the cattle drifted into the Sunbird herd. The weary cowboys dismounted at the corral, where the ranch-hand, Max Swilley, was waiting for news. He pushed back his battered Stetson and squinted at Jack.

'There was some feller here, lookin' for you, Jack. Said he'd be back. Looked an' sounded like trouble.'

'Booted an' suited trouble? Was he wearin' oddball duds?' Jack asked calmly, and Max nodded.

To Harry's deep satisfaction, Max baked a steak pie, with heavy gravy and a dish of fried, mixed vegetables. No one said much until they'd finished.

Then, full to bust, Harry pushed his chair slowly back from the table. 'We got to improve your chances o' gettin' elected, Jack,' he said. 'Bad news travels fast, an' it won't improve in the tellin'.'

Stern looked from Harry to Jack. 'We could hand the cattle over to anyone provin' ownership. Show we go with what's right.'

'Like hell we will,' Jack spouted. 'Those cattle were honestly bought an' paid for, with our money, your money. Waittes can go whistle Dixie.'

'You think maybe they're after takin' 'em?' Stern's voice turned curiously hopeful.

Harry chuckled. 'I think maybe they're goin' to try, Mister gunfighter.' He got up and moved towards the rear door. 'I'm takin' me a bed high in the barn. Remember, Gemson knows I'm here now, so they'll bring him.'

Harry strolled out to the corral. He pulled his saddle from the rail, and Max led off the horse. He climbed the hay

76

mow and lay between grain sacks in the open gateway.

Jack and Stern took seats on the porch. Stern had the Martini-Henry and Jack held a Winchester across his lap. Max lay out on a low bench in front of the bunkhouse, and Seth sat inside the house. He was facing the door with his Navy Colt balanced on the arm of his chair.

The waiting was broken by the soft rumbling of hoofs, west from the low bluffs. Jack and Stern flexed their fingers and Harry stared out from the barn. He called down to Max who reached for his scattergun and held it across his chest.

When the group of riders emerged from the sunset, Jack counted six, Gemson at the head and a stranger riding on the flank. With a lot of snorting and creaking of leather, the posse reined up to the ranch house. Gemson eased himself to the ground then strode up to acknowledge the two men on the veranda. 'Jack, Mr Stern.'

Stern said nothing, Jack spoke calmly. 'Evenin', Sheriff. Nice one for a ride.' He looked and nodded towards the stranger. 'Or for lettin' the new deputy see the effort needs to be put in hereabouts.'

The sheriff grunted. 'It'll be a bit o' both. I'm followin' up a report that there's Hangin' Gate cattle out here. I'm goin' to look over the herd you just bought in. You know I have to check it out, even if I know different. Lincoln Waittes told me it was Stern did the buyin'.'

Two men drew off from the group, dismounted and walked towards the corral. The hickory suited ramrod of the Hanging Gate turned and looked back at Jack. 'If there's stolen cattle, why not stolen horses?' he called out provocatively.

Stern looked at Jack, then at the ramrod. 'Because there ain't,' he snorted. 'Anythin' else on your mind, mister?'

'Harry Ridge maybe.' The man leered threateningly at Stern.

'This ain't *your* property, but we don't mind you lookin' over the stock,' Jack intervened to steady things down. 'If you've a mind for anythin' more though, you'll surely be lookin' to get them fancy duds messed up.'

The ramrod swore and made a move for his gun. But his hand had only moved a few inches when a rifle shot cracked the air. Dirt spat from between the man's boots, and a wisp of smoke drifted from the grain gate of the barn.

'That'll be the Ridges' guardian angel . . . again.' Jack shook his head and sighed.

'You idiot,' the sheriff hissed at the ramrod. 'You want to die over some stupid cows? Stern, show me your bill o' sale.'

Stern pulled out a crumpled piece of paper. The sheriff read it, and narrowed his eyes at the ramrod. 'It's good enough proof to a claim on the herd. An' it means we ain't found the stolen cattle we came here lookin' for.'

The ramrod of the Hanging Gate

turned on Jack and Stern. Jack appeared unmoved by his intimidation, but not Stern. 'This is my land an' my ranch. Now, I'm tellin' you: get out! Get off my property!'

But the ramrod was paying no heed. He lowered his head menacingly, sneered at Stern. 'An' I guess that's your *big gun*, too. Why, if you weren't holdin' it so tight, you'd more'n likely fall over.'

A tight, fleeting smile flared across Stern's face. He gently released his fingers from around the long barrel, let the rifle topple to the ground. 'I reckon an unarmed, one-legged hay slinger's about your equal,' he goaded.

The ramrod's eyes flicked with temper, and he drove in with a packed fist. Stern leaned, and struck at the man's head with a chopping drive. Before the man went down, Stern swore, and almost in surprise, smashed his bunched fist down on the back of the man's neck. As the man stumbled along on all fours, he stayed with him, pounded short, hammer blows into the meat of his sagging shoulders. The man tried to push himself up from his knees but failed, collapsed into the ground as another blow took him full and low in the back. With his fists still clenched tight, Stern took a pace back. He knew there was nothing more to do. He was distressed and his breathing came heavy. 'It's my leg that's bust', not my brain, or anythin' else, *Mr Johnnie Coxcomb*. Now ride off,' he rasped.

Seth Carlisle stepped down from the house. 'Someone sure don't need my learnin' any more,' he said with an appreciative wink towards Stern. He helped Jack pick up the beaten ramrod and together they set him slumped in his saddle.

'Best get yourselves away from here,' Jack looked tellingly at Gemson.

Gemson nodded, looked impressed and acknowledged Stern. 'Things ain't always what they seem, that's for sure,' he said, and glanced at the barn as the posse rode away.

7

Leading a plough mule, Jack rode to the foothills. He was uneasy about their captive in the line shack — the man whom Stern and Seth had transferred from the corn crib.

'We're in for a big rain,' he called out as he worked at opening the toughened door. 'A real goose-drowner.' He stepped back as he drew the door open, eyed the man coldly. 'The water comes roilin' through here waist high.'

The man was still milling for a fight, but the isolation had scratched his nerves. He blinked hard, looked uneasily at Jack. 'What's the point in leavin' me here?'

'It's a threat, goddamnit. I'll see no one comes through here for a month. Who paid you to kill me? Who is it wants me dead? Give me their name, an' you're free. St Louis's due east,

Springfield's a way south.'

Jack could see the breaking of resistance, the new uncertainty in the man's eyes. 'This squall's goin' to chase all sorts o' critters down from the timberline,' he pressed. 'If a grizzler gets mean an' hungry enough, it'll take more'n this door to stop him.'

Jack called the man's bluff. Wasting no more time, he shrugged and kicked the door to. But the man had already seen the menacing sky above the distant Ozarks. 'How far's Kansas City?' the man offered.

★ ★ ★

Jack's would-be killer was named Willard Sheet. Jack rode ahead of him, led them back to Sunbird's ranch house. Less than an hour later, Stern sat his horse atop the bluff, watched as Sheet rode north-west towards Sedalia and Kansas City.

★ ★ ★

Justice Durram read the confession that Jack had wrung from the hired killer, and advised a quick prosecution. 'The sooner the better, Jack. The county's been puttin' up with this sort o' thing for too long.'

But Jack wasn't sure. 'There's three others who are just as guilty as Gabriel Bonnet, Judge. If *he's* arrested, they'll run like hens from a rattler. Right now, they're all worried. The good sheriff's goin' to be wettin' himself tryin' to find Sheet . . . or his body. Can't you keep this quiet, until we get to the others? A sort o' *sub judice*?'

'That ain't exactly a ploy, Jack, an' it would be imprudent to wait,' the judge warned. 'The story of you rustlin' has spread wide. For those who don't know the truth, it's not exactly made you suited for office.'

Jack knew that, but more than collecting votes, he wanted to hold back Sheet's evidence against Bonnet. The judge acknowledged Jack's reckoning, and agreed to stow the signed statement provisionally.

The next day, Jack began to work at his campaign. He rode to neighbouring ranches, explained what he could and would do as sheriff.

Out at Raising Cayne, Nancy was mannerly and cool. Her father met him with a warning.

'There's moccasins in this town, son, an' they've found 'emselves a deep, dark pool. They're just waitin' for you to fall in.' He smiled thinly, as Jack took a seat on the porch.

'I know that, Mr Cayne. So I'm aimin' to shoot 'em from the bank.'

Cayne nodded gravely, then in what seemed a tactful gesture he went into the house. Jack turned to Nancy. 'Harvey must've told you about the fight we had,' he said. 'I couldn't do much about it. I don't know whether he told *you* that.'

Nancy looked him in the eyes. 'I think it would be much better for us all if you took the trouble not to come here again, Jack.'

'Obviously he didn't tell,' Jack responded.

He wanted to add that it was 'no trouble', but he quickly realized it wouldn't be what he meant. Nancy didn't know if what she'd just said would hurt, and Jack was in no mind to let her know if it did. So he said it with a smile.

'You do understand,' she said, just a mite thrown.

'Nope. It must be real inconvenient sometimes, to have Harvey as a brother.'

'What do you mean? Is there something else on your mind, Jack?'

'Yeah, there is. An' Harvey figures large. But at the moment I can't prove it.'

A cautious shadow darkened Nancy's features as she moved away. 'I'll tell my father you've left. Please don't come again.'

Jack thrust his feelings away, as he swung onto his horse. 'Won't even look back,' he muttered. He spurred deep and headed for Sunbird.

As he approached the ranch buildings, he heard the distant echo of gunfire from the east. He cursed loud and long as he levered shells into his Winchester. Then, gauging it to be the ramrod of the Hanging Gate come to collect his cattle, he kicked harder towards the guns.

Topping a low rise, Jack saw rising whorls of dust. The gunfire had died out, but he could hear the bellowing of cattle, and the rumble of their hoofs. He wasn't close enough to identify the outriders, but they weren't from Sunbird. One of them wheeled his horse, and came towards him at a dead run. He raised the Winchester and fired off a quick shot, but the rider came on. He levered another cartridge and took closer aim. This time the horse dropped to its knees, but the rider jumped clear. He took a running shot at Jack, then turned for his companions who were already into the valley.

Two riders came galloping back to cover. They slewed their mounts to bale up the man between them, then raced back to the rear of the herd. With the exception of a few stragglers, the cattle had run into the neck of a valley. Jack rode on, but couldn't understand why there was no sign of Stern, Seth or Max. And where was Harry? Single-handed, Jack wasn't going up against the men ahead of him.

A rifle bullet whined close to his shoulder and he fell to the neck of his horse. Grabbing the reins he rolled from his saddle into the cover of low brushwood. 'Doughboys never learn that move at West Point,' he huffed. 'Come on, Harry, look to your brother.'

Jack was wondering about his next move when, out of the valley a sudden burst of gunfire was followed by more bawling and bellowing. A wedged mass of cattle was struggling to turn in the valley, and from the wild look of the animals, Jack knew the leaders were being pressed hard by those behind. The crashing of the guns became louder and he saw three riders in the midst of the herd. They were trapped in a seething mass of hide and horn, frantically trying to stay in the saddle. One trip or stumble would mean dreadful injuries or death. The riders were firing back over the top of the herd.

'Hah, so that's where you are,' Jack reacted hoarsely.

Harry and Stern had turned the herd back into the rustlers. Max and Seth were following on, their faces tight-set with tension.

It was at that moment that the ramrod of Hanging Gate saw Jack. His gun swung up and a bullet smashed through the brush, then the whole herd thundered between them. Jack leaped to his horse and swerved away towards his partners. There was no need to continue the chase. The rustlers were making their retreat, had scattered with the cattle.

'You just got here in time,' Stern was grinning, rubbing the palm of his hand across his face. 'We sure raised some hair. We knew they'd come back, so we were ready,' Stern carried on, still keyed up and winded. 'We seen 'em roundin' up the herd. They were on my land . . . *our* goddamn land. We piled logs across the draw, an' when they drove up the valley we came at 'em from the flanks. Them ol' cows just turned and wanted home.'

Jack saw a trickle of blood from under Stern's hat. 'You hurt?'

Harry smiled at his brother. 'He got his brain box dented some. Ain't much left o' of the cow thief who did it. Ol' Onslow wanted to take 'em all on.'

Jack looked at Stern and puffed his cheeks tolerantly. 'Anyone else get hurt?'

Seth and Max shook their heads silently.

'How about them from Hanging Gate?'

Harry was still looking at his brother. 'You saw them that came out. We counted nine go in.'

'Christ, Harry. You didn't kill six of 'em?'

Harry looked serious. No. They

must've had an uprisin'. Two or three of 'em skittered out the other end o' the valley.'

Wearily, Jack squeezed his eyes shut. 'One of 'em came my way. He looked like the ramrod — Onslow's *coxcomb*. I couldn't make out the other two.'

'They'd be hired by Bonnet, though,' Harry said. 'Make us even more popular when him an' Gemson find out.'

Stern drew a dirty forefinger across his smear of blood. 'They'll all be runnin' scared from now on,' he crowed, and brandished the Martini-Henry.

Jack saw something in Onslow Stern's mood that worried him. The dashing, dangerous tomfoolery, a whiff of Harvey Cayne.

'Maybe we should ride into Come-back an' battle 'em,' was Harry's grumbled threat. 'We know who's behind it all.'

Jack was worried by the men's tangible irritation. 'We've got to wait

91

until I'm elected,' he told them. 'That way, whatever we do will be seen to be done right. An' *you*, Mr Stern, can keep that goddamn howitzer under control for a while longer.'

8

Harry and Stern were restless and edgy, needed something to sidetrack their pent-up frustrations.

'We could pussyfoot into town,' Stern suggested. 'We got to do somethin'.'

The pair took a wagon into Comeback, hitched outside of the Cooncan Saloon where they wanted some whiskey and a game of cards. They were standing at the bar joshing.

'Accordin' to Jack, they ain't got no likeness dodgers this side o' the lakes. So perhaps your notoriety ain't like real official,' Stern was suggesting jokily. The men were susceptible though, wary as Gabriel Bonnet was being told of them turning up.

Within moments, the saloon owner stormed from his office and made straight for Harry. 'I'll put it down to unmitigated stupidity, you comin' into town, Ridge. But this is my saloon, an' I want you to get the hell out o' here.'

Harry gave a thin, unfriendly smile. 'I can sort of understand your situation,' he said. 'But it's real surprisin' what a feller will play against, when he gets the boredom on him. You should be worryin' about how much help you're goin' to need, if we decide to stay awhile.'

It was Bonnet being pushed too far, and he glared at Harry, a tremor in his jaw. He took a backward step, and from within his frock coat, a silver-plated belly gun, appeared in his hand. 'You son-of-a-bitch, I'd goddamn sooner swing for this killin',' he rasped furiously.

Stern was standing just behind Harry. It was the position that a man with only one good leg takes to level a movement advantage. Quickly, he reached out and pulled the Colt from Harry's holster. In a smooth, rounded movement, he fired a single shot into Bonnet's coat. 'You'll be shot dead afore they get the rope around your neck,' he growled.

As Bonnet staggered, falling sideways against the bar, Harry grabbed his gun back from Stern.

'Now, we get the hell out o' here,' he advised.

They went for the swing door, but were stopped as Lambert Benk and Gemson pushed their way through. Harry was still holding his gun and he shoved it forward at Gemson.

'Sorry, Sheriff, this must be all your nightmares rolled into one. I swear as I'm standin' here with a gun in your gut, we only came into town for a drink an' maybe a few hands o' cooncan. 'Fraid I got to ask you an' Benk to step back outside.'

Stern took Benk's gun and together they walked the sheriff and town marshal to the jail. Benk was frightened speechless, Gemson faltered with incoherent rage. 'This'll add another foot to the height we're goin' to drop you from, Ridge,' he fumed.

Stern ordered them into a cell and tossed the keys into a half-full pail of wash water. Within minutes, they were racing their wagon from the end of town.

★ ★ ★

For three days Jack had been on his electoral campaign. It was while he was visiting one of the small, rawhide outfits, that he heard the news.

'Jack, my head's tellin' me to vote for you, an' I will; but I got to tell you, it's the other two's already got my gut vote.'

'What other two?'

'Stern, an' your brother. Like shootin' the flies from bad meat.'

'What the hell you talkin' about? What shootin'?'

'Christ, you ain't heard? Stern shot Gabriel Bonnet last night. In the saloon, less than ten feet from his own office.'

Jack was stunned, couldn't curse,

couldn't think. After a moment, he formed another basic question, but the rancher couldn't give him any more information.

★ ★ ★

Harry poured out the details, nodded in the direction of Stern as he tried an explanation. 'It was *his* idea. '*We just got to do somethin'*,' he said.'

Jack was hopping mad. 'Between you, you locked the town's peace officers in their own jail, an' I'm runnin' for county sheriff on the back o' new law an' order.'

Harry looked sheepishly at Stern. 'Yeah. I guess I should've stayed on the run.'

Jack looked up to the sky. 'That's just too good an idea for you to have had, Harry. Jeeez, what the hell do I do now?'

Harry's face took on some wily lightness. 'We'll do it for you, Jack. We'll both of us take the wagon up into the hills, an' this time I promise to stay lost.'

During the night, the sheriff failed to appear, and the following morning, Max Swilley rode to town. He discovered there was no warrant out for Harry or Stern, because Gemson was too busy acting out his own election show.

But that was all make-believe. If Jack got himself elected county sheriff, he'd have to arrest Harry *and* Stern. So, at the outset, there wasn't going to be a lot of fun in the job for him, and Gemson knew it.

★　★　★

Two days after that, not long after first light, Jack found Max and Seth getting ready to go to town. 'You boys are makin' a long day of it. Plenty o' time to put your marks alongside the name o' Jack Ridge,' he said.

Max looked at Seth, then back at Jack 'We were hopin' we'd be gone before — '

'Before what?' Jack interrupted, again fearful of the answer.

'Before we had to tell you they've gone an' robbed Lincoln Waittes. That new deputy was out here an hour ago. Somebody recognized Stern.'

'Robbed Waittes? Of what? What the hell are they doin'? They got cabin fevered on us?'

Max shrugged. 'Damned if I know. They were back here after midnight ... took the old prospector's wagon, an' didn't say where they were goin'.'

Jack left for town immediately, almost ran his horse into the ground in getting to the sheriff's office.

'You got a sandy craw ridin' in here,' Gemson scowled from behind his desk.

'Us Ridges need nerve just to breathe around these parts,' Jack retorted. 'I've just heard a wild tale. One o' the Sunbird boys says that Harry and Stern are accused o' holdin' up Waittes and his family, last night.'

Gemson leaned back in his chair. '*Wild* maybe, but they got the root of it.

99

An' if *you* win this election, *you'll* be bringin' 'em in. Sort o' poetic, ain't it?'

Jack walked to the door. 'Bonnet still clingin' to life, is he? Rats who've only got one hole, soon get caught, Sheriff.'

Gemson's boots fell to the floor. 'You go to hell,' he spat.

9

At midday Comeback was chock-full. The hitching rails and stables were packed with buckboards and horses. The town hadn't seen so much activity since Onslow Stern bought Sunbird Ranch.

Jack nudged his horse along a line of men at the polling station. 'Looks like the entire county's turned out,' he said.

'That's 'cause the entire county wants somethin' different,' Mole Painter answered back. 'Did you hear that Gabe Bonnet ain't goin' to die? Better that things won't be so hard for Stern when he's caught.'

Jack gave a non-committal nod, dismounted and pushed his way into the hotel.

Radford Carne moved away from a group of ranchers he was talking to. 'Congratulations, Jack. You've won, if all the talk means anythin'.'

Jack shook his head and smiled. 'Talk don't make the pot boil, Mr Cayne. I won't believe anythin' except the votes.'

Cayne frowned. 'It's bad news about Stern though. There were plenty o' witnesses besides the Feighs to testify that it was him an' Harry. Them two kicked the traces, ain't no mistake. Your brother must be really suited to deep water.'

Nancy arrived to join her father and Jack nodded politely. She stood to one side, watched the movement of the town impassively.

'What will you do about those two, if you're elected?' Carne asked. 'I mean, you'll be expected to go lookin' for 'em . . . bring 'em in. You'll do that?'

It was the one question Jack had been wondering himself. Any courtroom trial would be packed with jurymen influenced by Bonnet, one way or another. Jack narrowed his eyes and shrugged a response.

Jack glanced towards Nancy, and

Carne caught the look in his eye.

'She ain't been touched by the predicament o' family loyalty. Not yet, anyways. But that'll be for us to worry about, not *you*, Jack,' he said.

Before Jack had time to respond, Lincoln Waittes came in with his daughter. 'Sophie, this is Jack Ridge, the opposition candidate,' was his brusque introduction. 'He's tough and honest apparently, so be careful. In *these* parts, that's a commodity rarer than a water run.'

Jack was surprised at Waittes's droll humour, and would have had the daughter pegged wrongly as a chip off the old block.

'It's not a question of *opposition*, more like *best man for the work*,' he stated more pompously than he meant.

'I'm pleased to meet you, Mr Ridge. It's surprising that our paths have never crossed,' Sophie said, in the refined accent she'd brought all the way from her Baltimore education. 'Father tells me you too are a college man. I wasn't expecting to meet anyone of such a grade in this frightful territory.'

'And that could be why our paths have never crossed, miss,' Jack answered with his best winning smile. He was going to say more, but now Nancy was watching him, so he didn't make any further response.

Later, feeling sombre and oddly removed, he took a stroll to the Cooncan. He saw two of Bonnet's men elbowing their way excitedly into the street and he speculated on the reason. As the afternoon wore on, he saw more of Bonnet's employees riding off. They were all stirred-up by something, and Jack's puzzlement turned to irritation. 'A sheriff benefits to know these things,' he muttered thoughtfully.

By evening, the town was back to its usual, regular pace. Jack was talking over the day's events to Lambert Benk. 'There's somethin' in the wind, that's for sure,' he suggested.

The town marshal grinned slyly. 'I reckon they know it's you goin' to get elected. So they won't be drawin' the attention o' your pistol, that's a cert.'

Jack gave him a wry look. 'Funny ol' way o' goin' about it,' he said, as he walked away from the jail.

At the sheriff's office, he remarked about the same thing to Gemson.

'Yeah, I'd be fearful o' you throwin' me into one o' Benk's cells,' Gemson sniggered.

Next, Jack found Mole Painter and told him of his unease.

'It *is* odd,' the rancher agreed. 'Suspicious, too. I'll see if Lemmy knows what's goin' on.'

Jack had sent Seth back to the Sunbird with Max, who was a bit peeved at having to depart the festivities so early.

Now, he was sitting at a single table in the hotel, forking his meal. 'Just pretend I'm not here, why don't you?' he said, in between quickly swallowing his chicken pieces. The harmonica player and two fiddlers were in the dining room irritatingly tuning their instruments. 'Take more'n a goddamn tune to get me skippin' lightly,' he muttered.

★ ★ ★

The townsfolk had gathered to hear the election returns, but mostly for the hoedown. Women were in their best homespuns or flower-printed, store-bought dresses. Men with guns and spurs had prudently hung them up. Their hair was plastered tight with grease, and smelled of cheap pomade.

It was in the middle of a lively stomp when a cowboy ran into the hotel and yelled, 'Jack Ridge has been elected. He's our new county sheriff.'

There was an immediate cheer and a round of applause, then some really hearty back-slapping and handshaking. A cowboy weaved his way through the congratulating dancers and got as close to Jack as he could. 'Friend o' yours out back . . . wants to see you,' he confided, in a croaky whisper.

Fending off new-found supporters, Jack threaded his way out of the hotel. He followed the man into an alley and Onslow Stern emerged from the darkness.

He grabbed Jack by the arm and spoke hurriedly. 'We got to be quick,' he started anxiously. 'Me an' Harry seen Bonnet's men dammin' up the Moss-bank. The water'll start headin' south along the old bed. We're goin' to be dry as grandpa's bones. It was just chance that we saw 'em.'

Jack swore, looked hard at Stern. 'There's some goddamn mean work goin' on here, Onslow. Take Max an' get us some help. There shouldn't be a shortage of any. I'll deputize anyone who can put one foot in front of another, if I have to. An' take dynamite. That's *our* land.'

A moment or two later, Jack heard Stern's horse pounding away. He saw Mole Painter outside the hotel and told him what he'd heard, what was going on.

Soon, worried, angry ranchers were leaving the dance. While the women made the drive back to their ranches, the men rode for the hills in a fearsomely angered group.

Gemson, Waittes and Radford Cayne accompanied Jack to Justice Durram's house, where Jack impatiently accepted and read out the oath of his new office. Waittes looked curiously pleased as he waited, then full of himself as he drew an envelope from his pocket and handed it to Jack.

'This is the authority that approves the construction of that dam. Have a read, Sheriff.'

Jack felt his stomach muscles writhe. *This* is the clever little 'cloud buster' that Waittes had in mind, he thought as he read the document. The banker had totally disregarded the Ridge family's lease, and somehow obtained legislative consent for the dam. He handed it to the judge. 'Is this genuine?' he asked hollowly.

Justice Durram nodded. 'The authority to build is. He couldn't live with the trouble if it weren't.'

Cayne had been watching the new sheriff. 'That's a tough one to enforce Jack,' he said. 'It'll ruin Sunbird an' four or five other ranches, an' I knew nothin' of it.'

When the others had left, their business done, Jack stood quiet. He felt the law pressurizing him, and Justice Durram looked regretful. 'Short term, there ain't much we can do, Jack. An injunction would require that the owner puts in an appearance.'

Jack slumped his shoulders and studied the floor around his boots. He'd just sent Sunbird's new owner off with a sackful of stump dynamite.

Durram had a stab at expressing Jack's predicament. 'There's a narrow margin between justice an' the law, Jack. Presently, you got yourself squeezed in there real tight.'

Jack nodded with full appreciation of the judge's summary. 'I expect you know how I'm goin' to handle this, Judge,' he said. 'If I'm goin' to break the law, I might as well do it lawfully. As for the 'narrow margin' you're talkin' about? I'm about to fill it, an' I'll goddamn use the bodies of those who try an' stop me.'

Jack stormed off to the jail. Lambert Benk had been playing clock patience, and he was sitting drowsy, snoring in his chair. Jack lashed out with his boot.

Shaken, Benk scrambled to his feet. 'Wha . . . what is it . . . what do you want?' he stuttered.

Jack ripped the badge from the man's vest. 'You're on too many payrolls. An' I don't like you, an' I didn't appoint you. Come back in the mornin' and draw your pay. Now get out.'

From the jail, he went to the saloon and found the man he was looking for. 'Crewes, I'm in no mood to waste time,' he said. 'I'm told you're reliable, a man of integrity. Well, right this moment, they're qualifications I'm sorely in need of, together with a town marshal. Will you do *that*?'

Maitland Crewes was the town's colossus of a smith. 'Will I? Ha, just give me a chance, Sheriff,' he boomed. 'That's a civic improvement I can build up . . . make somethin' of.'

For a fleeting moment, Jack wondered if he'd done the right thing. However, he shook hands on the deal for immediate effect.

Outside of the livery stable, Jack found his new deputy, the man whom Crewes recommended. Crick Olland was a friendly young cowhand, enthusiastic and willing to try anything.

They rode to the Sunbird and Jack spoke to Seth Carlisle. He explained what was going on up at the timberline, and with a few reservations asked him to stay at the ranch. They took coffee, but in less than an hour Jack and Olland were set for the foothills. They rode fresh horses and they racked through the arid gullies that led to the high course of the Mossbank.

Olland was peering up to the first of the pine stands. 'What you figgerin' to do when we get to that dam, Sheriff? Folk are mighty proddy at this water business, an' that was a big gather of anger that left town.'

Jack gently nudged his horse. 'I'll show 'em what happens when Comeback's recently elected sheriff gets proddy,' he said, smiling wryly at his deputy.

10

The air was clean and cold, and they'd used waning moonlight to travel by. Crick Olland had been chary, didn't like night sounds and the dark with its formless shadows. The two men climbed through the timberline, their horses' hoofs clicking and rattling against the scree. Stern had told Jack the approximate location of the dam, and they headed to the nearest run of water.

Crick slouched in his saddle. 'Lack of sleep must be gettin' to me. I've been dreamin' of hot peach cobbler. We takin' a meal camp before we get there?' he asked tiredly.

'I know you mean well, Crick, but I got a bit more to worry about than your bread bin,' Jack snapped back. He stared ahead of him grimly as they picked their way along the shale bed of the watercourse, the cold water sucking and swirling at the feet of their horses. When they could no longer follow the course of the stream, they climbed out through a pine-covered ridge, and Jack nodded towards the gully below.

'There it is. Stern was right. It ain't much, but it's good enough to divert the water.'

'Yeah, but it looks a bit too quiet,' Crick suggested.

They close-hauled the horses with tight reins and slanted cautiously down the side of the gully.

As if from waiting, Gemson appeared from behind the great root ball of a blown pine. He was closely followed by Harry, then an anxious-looking Mole Painter.

'Mornin', Sheriff,' Harry yelled. 'You got the full weight o' the law ridin' with you?'

Gemson turned to face Painter and Harry. 'He sure has, but not in the way you're thinkin' boys. The good sheriff's here to protect the dam. We got the legislature consent to build.'

Jack sighed, was interested in Gemson's use of the word 'we'.

Then Painter shouted, 'We're ready to blow this heap o' garbage apart, Jack. Just say the word.'

Stern was standing behind and to one side of Harry and Painter. He read the unusual resignation of Jack's features and edged back into dense fern.

'I never knew it at the time, but I was wrong,' Jack said, as evenly as he could. 'An' Gemson's right. They got 'emselves a document from Jefferson City. You got to back off, leave the dam be.'

Harry turned to his brother. 'You're lettin' 'em get away with a goddamn piece o' paper?'

Jack nodded. 'Yeah, it's the law, Harry. It's either with you, or it ain't. An' right now, *they* got it.'

While Gemson smirked, Stern had worked his way to within a few feet of one end of the dam. The ranchers had emerged from cover. They were waving their gun barrels at the ground, shuffling their feet around Harry and Painter, waiting on the next move.

Stern was hunkered down watching Gemson and the men who'd put up the dam. He let his hand drop to the ground, and casually flared a match on a stone beside his foot. Then he glanced sideways quickly and scrambled to his feet. 'Run for it,' he yelled. 'I've gone an' lit the goddamn fuse.'

Gripping their guns, men ran for cover, dived to safety. But Jack and his deputy were caught in a deadly cross-fire. Rifle shots reverberated through the gully, more gunfire crashed and bounced off the surrounding rocks and timber.

As Crick Olland fell from his horse and crawled for shelter, Jack was watching a trail of smoke as it spitted along the lighted fuse. Then, in spite of the assault of bullets, he kicked his heels and sprang forward, stamped at the fizzing flame with the hoofs of his horse. He cursed loudly, and wheeled away, reached out for Olland's shotgun. He fired off both barrels and through the echoes and holding silence, yelled for everyone to cease firing. As the noise faded, Stern appeared, grinning from behind a pile of timber props and ties. But there was something wrong and, as Jack watched, the man's grin stretched into a tight grimace. Stern was faltering from more than a busted leg, and Jack started running, swore at the stain that welled darkly across the front of Stern's shirt. Stern crumpled to the ground, and fell onto his side, his sight drifting slowly across the mud-slicked grass.

Harry came up and reached out his hand to his brother's shoulder, but Jack said nothing. There was no need. They both understood. Onslow Stern had wanted some excitement in his life. He'd got that — bought it by buying Sunbird. If he hadn't, they'd all probably be making out in tent city or punching other people's cows by now. And he wasn't much on sentimentality, didn't even take to his own name. Max Swilley brought a canteen of water and held it to his lips. But nothing moved, and Stern's eyes weren't seeing any more.

One of the ranchers laid a Navajo blanket beside Jack. 'Can we get him back to town . . . to the doc?' he asked.

Before Jack could say no, a strident voice called out to them.

'If he'd knocked out that dam, I'd have stuffed his goddamn leg into the next one. You hear me, Sheriff?'

Other than someone swearing, the silence was pulverizing as Jack and Harry turned towards Gemson. But, affected by the tinderbox atmosphere, the brothers remained very still and Gemson carried on living.

There was sudden fear among the ranchers and the men building the dam. One or two of them had been at the Cooncan when Jack shot Hawker Bream, remembered the way the Ridge brothers dealt with retribution. It created a situation where neither camp wanted to push either their predicament or their gunfighting.

Max suggested hauling the body back, but they all knew the terrain down from the timberline was impassable for a travois. Jack's alternative was a short prayer, with words for dead soldiers, and they used it to bury Stern. It was beside a bright, gurgling headwater above a ridge that overlooked the Sunbird ranch. Soon after, the ranchers left for their homes. Onslow Stern had never meant much to them until now, until he'd given his life for their right to water. But for most of the smaller ranchers, the death blow was upon them. It looked like the alliance had gained a stranglehold on the entire county, and many of them were already voicing their regret at voting for Jack Ridge. They thought he'd be with them, regardless.

★ ★ ★

Justice Durram listened with exasperation and sadness to the account of the gunfight and Stern's death. When Jack

119

had finished, he handed him a flat, wrapped package.

'He asked me to hold these letters for you, Jack. It was in the event of his death. You see, the ranch never really belonged to him. Harry's the inheritor . . . always was. Stern just paid the money. If Harry dies, or what's increasingly more likely, gets himself killed, it all goes to you. The Newburg City Bank's holdin' the will and some other documents.'

Jack walked back to the sheriff's office. He unlocked the door, went in, and locked it again from the inside. He pushed open the door to his own bunk room and looked grimly at his brother.

'Best be on my way,' Harry said, after quickly reading through Stern's letters. 'You'll have to start servin' them warrants soon.' He stood and rubbed the arm of his shirt across Jack's badge of office. 'An' by the way, those papers me and Stern took from Waittes? They're probably still in his saddle pouch. They meant nothin' to me, but he thought different. Find 'em and have a look.'

'I will. Where you goin', Harry?'

The reluctant fugitive smiled sourly. 'I promised to give you a free rein, Jack. But now they killed Stern, all that's changed. If you need help, see Max. He'll be able to find me. An' keep an eye on the ranch. It really does belong to *me*, don't forget.' Harry grabbed his brother by the shoulders and shook him gently. Within a minute or so was gone.

Jack stepped back into the office and turned over the contents of Stern's saddle pouch. Then for a long time he stood at the window, looked thoughtfully towards the setting sun. Later he had two visitors. They were Tayler Gemson, and a more than usually portentous Lincoln Waittes.

'We're approving of your actions at the timberline, Sheriff,' he started, 'but we ought to make it quite clear, there are one or two other things you should be considering.'

It was all Jack could do to stop

himself laying in to the pair of them, there and then. The banker sensed it, flushed up a little and blustered. 'There's warrants out, and you know who you should be bringing in. Are you doing something about it?'

Jack smiled icily. 'Yeah, I know who I should be bringin' in all right. Your scum payroll.'

Gemson twitched as Jack contemptuously spat his words. 'I was elected on a platform o' law an' order. So, if my brother shows up, I'll take him in, or try to. But, by the same token, maybe I'll finish cleanin' out the Cooncan. Now there's one or two things for you an' your cronies to consider.'

Waittes nodded. '*Touché*, Sheriff. Comeback will be well rid of the trash you're alluding to.'

Jack pulled his gun. '*Alludin' to*, my ass. You're the sort we'll all be well rid of, Waittes. I'd empty every jail in the county in exchange for bangin' up you two.' The sheriff pushed his gun deep and low into Waittes's stomach as he spoke. With his other hand he grabbed at Gemson's throat, looked him in the eye. 'Get out o' here, Gemson. An' take this stuck pig with you. Start prayin' they don't catch up with Harry. 'Cause if they do, an' somethin' happens to him, there ain't nothin' in Christendom that'll stop me reachin' you.'

When the two men had gone, Jack waited for his blood heat to drop. It was full dark now, and the peaks of the Ozarks were as black as the night. 'What to do now, eh, Onslow?' He pondered quietly. 'You'd probably've shot 'em both.'

11

In a bleak mood, Jack rode out to Raising Cayne. He cracked his heels across the timbers of the stoop as a severe notice of his calling.

Radford Cayne came to the door and met Jack with a look of welcome. 'Hello Jack. It's late, is there somethin' wrong?'

'Yeah, there is. It's about Onslow Stern.'

Nancy came from another room, stepped up beside her father. She saw the cloud in Jack's eyes and immediately looked to Cayne for a response.

The rancher put out a hand for Jack to enter the house. 'Stern? What about him? Come in.'

Jack pulled off his hat and ran the brim between his fingers. 'I told him to organize the ranchers and dynamite the dam. But there was somethin' I didn't know at the time, an' because of it he died. That's wrong an' regretful, Mr Cayne. I just came to tell you.'

'I think that's only half the reason,' Nancy spoke up. 'Sunbird becomes yours again, doesn't it? You came to remind us.' There was no sympathy in her voice as she turned her back and walked from the room.

'Not long ago, someone told me they thought this was frightening territory, Mr Cayne. If it is, I'm suspectin' it's the *people* that make it that way,' Jack retorted bitterly.

As Jack climbed onto his horse to leave, a figure approached the hitching rail.

'Tough on your man Stern, Sheriff. Did they shoot him or fell him?'

As Jack looked down at Harvey Cayne, his mind angled for an appropriate response. If there'd been a simple one, it would have been the end of Cayne there and then. Cayne knew it and gritted his teeth. He backed off slowly, held his hands out to Jack to acknowledge his reckless and malicious stupidity. Jack wondered if many folk knew for certain when they were within a second or two of dying. He held up his hand, showed Cayne the small gap between his forefinger and thumb. 'That far, sonny,' he rasped. 'That far.'

★ ★ ★

Mole Painter had suggested a service for Stern. 'Black robes got 'emselves a heap o' work in this neck o' the woods,' he suggested, when they'd waited nearly a week for the travelling minister. The short ceremony was held outside the hotel and a few ranchers came to pay their late respects.

Shortly after the bank clock had struck midday, Jack caught sight of Harry sidling his horse in from the end of town. Others saw it too, and they looked to him for a response.

Gemson and Waittes stepped to the balustrade that fronted the hotel, and Jack cursed out his annoyance.

'Arrest him, Sheriff,' Gemson goaded.

Harry dropped from his horse and looked around him warily. He pulled a Winchester from his saddle sheath and, while looking at Gemson, spoke quietly. 'Whatever you heard or seen lately, Stern was a real peaceable fellow. So, for the sake o' his respect, I'm warnin' you to keep your mouth shut tight,' he warned. 'Max, take his gun, and look to the banker. Jack, give your gunbelt to Seth.'

Gemson's face purpled with rage as Max and Seth stepped forward, and Waittes puffed with indignation as Max prodded at him.

'Could hide a goddamn army in this lot,' Max remarked, at Waittes's slack belly fat.

The ranchers shuffled uneasily, and Harry gave a challenging look to Gemson and Waittes as they backed into the hotel. The minister had been waiting uneasily, but as soon as he'd offered a hurried prayer, the ranchers began to drift off.

'Sorry 'bout the gun, Jack,' Harry said. 'But thought I was in danger o' bein' arrested. I need to talk to you without that.'

The small group walked to the corral and Harry beckoned to Mole Painter. He took Jack's gunbelt back from Seth. 'That was for appearance.' He winked at his brother. 'I've been back to the dam. They've finished buildin' and the water's reachin' for the old channel. In a week, the range's goin' to be dried up, an' in less than a month, the herds will be dyin'. I'm concerned about more than Sunbird . . . wondered what you had in mind.'

Jack held the palm of his hand to a nosing mule. 'Not much. They'd got authority to build that dam. Justice Durram says he can go higher than state legislature, but it may be weeks before we get an overturn.'

Mole Painter nodded gloomily. 'I'm goin' to dig myself a well.'

'Hell, Mole, you never heard o' pissin' in the wind?' Harry burst out.

'Your cattle will be dead before you've mucked enough for your own grave.'

Jack watched the mule as it stomped the hard-packed dirt. Not quite so suddenly, he was regretting that he was sheriff. He aimed to give the weaker ranchers some legal support, had told them so. But the law was creating barriers, had become rigid, near brittle. 'Harry, you promised you'd give me a free hand, if and when I was elected,' he said. 'I hope you meant it.'

Harry laughed. 'I did, Brother. But let's hope we hear somethin' in a month. After that, I'll go and blow the dam myself. We all got four weeks, Jack.'

Painter nodded in agreement. 'That's fair, Sheriff. The herds can just about make it for that long.'

The five men walked back to the hotel and Harry smiled wistfully as he handed back Jack's gunbelt.

'Just remember, Jack,' he said. 'Life's a bubble on the stream. That's *our* life an' *our* stream.' Moments later he rode from town. He was headed north, and Jack was headed back to his office.

★ ★ ★

For the next week, Jack was too busy with parochial duties to give any particular attention to the ranchers' water plight. With the help of Crick Olland, and the enthusiastic town marshal, Maitland Crewes, Comeback made a start on its civic clean up. Gemson kept out of his way, as did Gabriel Bonnet who'd recovered from his shooting by Stern.

He'd seen little of the banker, but one afternoon Sophie stopped him on the street, and chided him for not paying her a visit. Unlike her father, she was open, genuinely interested in Jack's obligations as sheriff.

'Right now, I can't do much, 'cause my deputy's off to Springfield. 'Quotidian Duties', is how the employer's agreement refers to it,' Jack was saying, as they took to the sidewalk.

Sophie smiled innocently. 'I've never known a sheriff before. Not one to walk with, anyway. You're not a bit like I imagined.'

'I can't think what you might mean by that, Sophie. Wager I ain't much like the shootists in them dime-novels you probably got secreted in your Baltimore dorm'.'

They'd walked to his office and Jack looked around him. 'An' very few of us become as wealthy as your father,' he continued. 'Not unless we use the trappin's of office to get an advantage.' He looked at her with as much cynism as he dared. 'There's disease an' rustling, an' drought takes a big toll. As for the law, if I can't get water down to the ranches in a couple o' weeks, there's some who'll start dispensin' their own.'

'You're talking of your brother, aren't you? And why do you hate my father so?'

'I don't *hate* him, Sophie. It's a genuine an' sincere disgust. An' it's for *all* carpetbaggers an' profiteers. That's strong I know, an' I'm sorry. But it's one o' the things I was learning at West Point. How to help put an end to the speculation and subsequent fighting, war even. Your father an' his colleagues — his *alliance* — only have a profit interest in this land, land that my father an' folk like him, gave their lives for.'

'I don't understand,' Sophie said. 'How does my father make a profit from the ranchers having no water?'

'If the cattle don't get water, the ranchers are forced to sell up. The water's rerouted, and he ends up ownin' half the county that he's bought at bottom dollar. But this time, Sophie, I ain't seein' what my pa died for, end up as *your* pa's gain.'

★   ★   ★

The next morning Jack rode north through the bluffs, then he dropped to the sage flats of the Painter spread. The lack of water had already crazed the land, and with the aid of his wife and a cow hand, Mole was toiling in the parched soil. When Jack rode up, his rheumy eyes brightened.

'Any news, Sheriff?' he asked hopefully.

Jack shook his head. 'None that would be true, Mole.'

'Then Harry was right,' the old rancher niggled. 'We should've fought it out.' He kicked at a piece of loose timber, the likely structure of a bore hole. 'Two weeks we been workin' at this. There's more of our goddamn sweat down here than water.'

Jack didn't want to say that if it had been that easy, they'd all have sunk wells, years ago.

At Suggets Bend, the situation was just as bad. But, Hamilton Sugget wasn't up for any alternative to a fight. Jack tried to assure him that guns weren't the answer, but after only five minutes, he knew he wasn't going to convince the man.

When Jack recrossed the bluff, he would have been more worried if he'd turned and seen the activity around the ranch. Two men rode off bristling with rifles and shotguns, and Sugget drove horses in from the home pasture. A coaster was loaded with provisions and canvas pokes were bundled up and securely tied to the flanks of two rimrock mules. They were plugged with saddle blankets to bolster any shaking, then covered with oilskin.

12

Another day on, and Jack was riding south with his deputy. They stopped at the Raising Cayne ranch where they were met by the foreman, Amos Heron.

'Have you boys been seein' much from the Mossbank? It's sure hard on your old Sunbird, but to us, that water's manna from heaven,' he said needlessly, but without ill will.

Jack and Olland rode until they crossed the new course of the Mossbank. There was a head of water in the stream and it was flowing swiftly towards the Hanging Gate and ranches beyond. A green carpet was rolling across the land as the grasses fattened with moisture.

At the Hanging Gate, the ramrod walked across the yard to intercept them at the corral. Jack noticed how their cattle had taken on weight since his last visit. 'Ain't exactly a half-starved herd o' dogies,' he suggested drily.

The suited man agreed and laughed. 'Must be all that spring water sloshin' around in their bellies,' he said, but didn't meet Jack's eye.

Jack swung his horse's head away, once again considered the iniquity of crime and punishment. These were the men who felt nothing for the land or cattle, and there was no effective law against it.

★　★　★

Saturday in Comeback, but only the Cooncan House and the hotel were lit for business.

'Where are they all?' Crick Olland asked. 'There'd be more life in Boot Hill, if we'd got one.'

With no more than a dozen horses on the street, Jack *had* noticed the quietness. Finding that Maitland Crewes was not at the jail, they strolled to the saloon.

Gabriel Bonnet was standing at the

bar, and he turned to face the lawmen. 'What the hell you done to this town, Ridge? I've never known the place so dead.'

Jack shook his head. 'I was goin' to ask you the same thing. Maybe it's the trouble on the timberline.'

They heard a horse snorting and pounding outside the saloon. 'Someone's heard there's a party somewhere,' Olland muttered, 'or been to one . . . let's go.'

The two men reached the sheriff's office as a rider dismounted and stumbled to the ground. Together they grabbed at his long duster, and carried him inside. He'd taken a bullet in his right shoulder and Olland ran for Doc Pagham, the town doctor.

Jack wanted to know what trouble the rider had brought with him, and persuaded the doctor not to administer any laudanum. But before Pagham began his probe for the bullet, the man's eyes opened and he looked up into Jack's face.

'They're razin' the dam, Sheriff. Gemson's holed up in the gully, an' there's no way out,' the man garbled weakly. 'Some of 'em are hurt worse'n this. Leave me some snake-head, an' take the doc with you.'

Jack asked Olland to find fresh horses. He hurried to the hotel, and then the saloon, seeking to make up a posse. But the few able bodies who were left in town weren't disposed to a gunfight.

'I could've got you some men, if you hadn't thrown your weight around in here. You're a shirt-tail-sheriff,' Bonnet sneered.

Outside the Cooncan, Jack gave an inscrutable look to the bright, blue sky that mantled the timberline. 'An' there's me thinkin' there just might be a God,' he said.

He didn't waste any more time and, with Olland, rode to the west of Sunbird then on to the Ozark foothills. It was reminiscent of when they'd first rode to the dam, except this time it was a waxing moon that lit their way.

Doc Pagham had been slow and they hadn't waited. He could be an hour's ride behind them. Eventually the moon dropped and shadows merged into the blackness ahead of them. Olland was his usual nervy disposition, but he kept quiet and for another three hours they climbed steadily upward. It wasn't until the dawn sky broke, that they drew in their horses.

In the gully, the dam was clouded in low swirling mist. There was someone hidden high on the ridge, and his voice cut the crisp, still air. 'It's the sheriff. They can see us but they can't stop us. Spray that dam.'

The gunfire erupted along the gully, rasping and clattering among the rock strewn walls. And from the barrier of the dam came the returning volley of bangs and flashes.

'We ain't come to help 'em. Why the hell did they wait?' Olland yelled.

Jack seemed unperturbed as he looked across the gully and down to the dam. 'Yeah, I wonder. First light maybe? Nothin' much for us to do but sit an' do the same,' he said.

They dismounted, tied their horses into the pines and Jack hunkered to consider the crossfire. Don't go through it, was his first thought. That sort of thing's best left to the likes o' Lord Cardigan an' his Scots Greys. Then he recalled the voice they'd heard from the ridge. It was Hamilton Sugget.

The light spread, but mist still pushed and eddied its way into the narrow gully. Jack stood, took a reckoning look around him. 'The doc should be near,' he said. 'Take a walk back an' see. I'll go find a skunk hole . . . flush out Gemson.'

Olland voiced his concern. 'I wouldn't. I heard that Onslow Stern caught a stray bullet.'

Jack gave Olland a sharp look. 'Hardly a stray,' he said. 'I hope I didn't make a mistake with you, Deputy. Get goin'.'

Jack edged his way along the gully.

Through the mist, a bullet ricocheted and whined by his ear. He ducked on impulse, his foot slipped, and he tumbled into a boulder. As his rifle fell to the stream, Sugget and Mole Painter emerged from the swirling bank-side mist. Sugget stepped down into the water and retrieved the Winchester, then he lifted Jack's revolver from his holster.

'Not quite the slip we been waitin' on, Sheriff,' he said, smiling thinly. 'But this is our little ceremony, so you get back to the ridge while we just blue ticket the dam.'

Painter motioned with his Colt, and Sugget looked back along the stream bed and across the gully. 'An' where's that deputy o' yours?' he queried. 'We were expectin' two o' you.'

Jack splashed from the shallow water. 'Believe me, he won't be too far away. Is my brother with you?'

'He ain't no part o' this. He promised to stay away,' Painter reminded Jack.

Jack knew that Harry would keep his

141

word about how long he'd stay away. But as he scanned the timber and rocks above him, he wondered just how far it would be. He turned to Painter. 'Mole, you know the law,' he started. 'Goddamnit, you elected me to enforce it, or what there was of it. What's the point of all that, if you're goin' vigilante?'

The rancher shook his head slowly, looked across at Sugget. 'I'd rather go to jail for doin' somethin' rather than the grave for doin' nothin'. An' that goes for all of us. You can watch from the ridge, Jack. Right now, you don't have too much say.'

Jack was about to move on Painter's offer when four figures emerged from the trees. Behind Olland and Doc Pagham two men were following closely with lowered rifles.

Olland leered at Painter and Sugget, then he looked resignedly at Jack. 'You get the feelin' we ain't wanted here, Sheriff? Why the hell don't we let 'em slug it out?'

The doc set to tending the wounded,

and Jack and his deputy were led back to the ridge. As the sun climbed higher it burned off the mist and the shooting broke out again.

'How many men's Gemson got?' Jack asked.

'A dozen . . . I'm not sure. They're scattered.' Mole Painter swung the tip of his rifle up to the peaks. 'With the high rain from last week, there's a head o' water on the way. There's already some depth in the old channel, so that dam's got to go now, if it's goin'.'

Jack realized why. When the Mossbank threw its course, it would have to be dammed again, to throw it back. He squatted on the ridge and watched the fight below. If Gemson had started with ten men, he didn't have more than seven now, probably less. There wouldn't be a long wearing down, and there would be no reinforcement.

The sun's heat was starting to build. It didn't distress the ranchers much, hidden among the pine and rocky fissures of the gully, but it was pitiless to those defenders in and around the dam. This is what battles used to be like, Jack mused. The opposing generals watching the cut and thrust from convenient vantage points, often cheered on by their wives and lovers. Between offensives, and from beneath campaign shades, they would glide among tables that groaned with cold cuts, egg custards and sparkling wines.

Jack was going to ask if Olland had brought any food supplies with him, but thought better of it. Instead, he told Painter that he wanted to speak to Hamilton Sugget. 'Can you get him up here quickly?' he asked.

Fifteen minutes later a cowhand returned with Sugget. 'I'm talkin' more'n the law, now,' Jack said and pointed into the gully. 'There's three o' Gemson's men down there, an' they're wounded. If they're left any longer we'll smell 'em from up here. Send someone to bring 'em out. Them an' the doc. You're no killer, Sugget, an' there's no future in becomin' one. So just do it.'

A withering fire started to pound the dam, and under its cover, a small group of men were slanting their way down the gully. Trying to reach the dam, one of the ranchers clutched a handful of short-fused dynamite. He got to within thirty feet of the barrricade, before Gemson's men managed to rip their bullets into him. The rancher went down but, as he hit the ground he rolled, slowly raised himself to one knee and bowled the deadly package into a high curling flight. One stick fell short into the stream, the other two hit the ground before bouncing between fissures in the stacked timbers. No one was killed, or anyone else injured, but the blast was enough to send up a mighty scattering of water, wood, stones and mud. A trickle of muddied water began to ooze, then more, until the stream began to muscle its way between the tangle of logs and broken timbers. A final fusillade broke against the dam, but it was overwhelmed by the triumphant yells that broke from the ranchers.

Jack heard, then saw Sugget who started shouting and pointing. A rider was coming along the stream and Jack made out the glint of a marshal's star against a dark mackinaw shirt. Four men were following on, and Jack recognized them immediately. They were Radford Cayne and his foreman Amos Heron, Seth Carlisle and Justice Durram.

Hamilton Sugget sloshed down the stream to meet them, and Jack saw him shake hands with the marshal. With Mole Painter still close, Jack and Olland were escorted down to the bed of the gully.

'Good mornin' to you, Sheriff,' the marshal greeted Jack. 'Gregor Poe, US Marshal all the goddamn way from Springfield.'

Jack looked into a brutally hard face, took immediate note of the marshal's innate command.

'Judge here's got a rescind order

from a Government Land Office,' Poe stated. 'Bottom line authorizes me to blow up some pesky water boom. I've already had me enough of a hard-assed time, so if we're here, you can get on with it.'

The men started to move away from the wrecked dam. '*We're* here all right, Marshal, but *you're* too late. These range bums have gone an' stole your thunder,' Tayler Gemson answered back.

For a moment all the opposing factions sat and watched splintered debris, as water flowed back to the old stream bed.

The marshal took a deep breath. 'I did wonder what all the noise was about,' he said, returning his attention to Jack. 'Whoever's responsible for this was askin' for trouble, but I ain't takin' anyone back to Springfield with me.' Then he looked sternly at Hamilton Sugget. 'But that don't mean that some-one ain't gettin' their wick trimmed.'

'There's more than one man already paid the price, Marshal. Others will too,' Jack assured Poe. He had his gunbelt returned, and wearily he mounted his horse. He exchanged quick words with the marshal who nodded in agreement.

Jack stood his stirrups, the marshal on one side and Olland on another. He held up his hand until the men quietened right down. 'The water's runnin' back to your ranches, but there's a price to be paid,' he told them. 'Hand over your guns an' gunbelts to Deputy Olland.'

Mole Painter was the first to respond. 'You ain't takin' *me* to jail, Sheriff,' he challenged.

Marshal Poe's Colt suddenly appeared in his hand and Jack smiled grimly. 'Most o' you here are my friends an' neighbours. So, I've asked the marshal to shoot the first man who makes a move for his gun. He assures me he will, 'cause he can do it legal, an' he's a tired, fractious son-of-a-bitch.'

It wasn't a bluff but a threat, and not worth resisting, and the ranchers and cowhands dropped their handguns and rifles to the ground.

During the surrender, a large muscle of a man eased off from the group and slipped almost unnoticed into the surrounding timber. It was Jack who saw him, but he gave no sign. The man was Maitland Crewes, the town marshal. Once upon a time, he'd been a top hand at the Sugget Bend ranch. It was his regard for his former employer that had brought him into the fight, but he wasn't after compromising Jack Ridge, or losing his new job.

13

Under the watchful eye of the sheriff and the US marshal, a hangdog bunch of men rode down from the timberline that same day's afternoon. Comeback's jail was small and already occupied, and Jack settled for holding three ranch owners. The hands returned to their ranches, but they had Jack's warning ringing in their ears for a reappearance. Gregor Poe overnighted to catch the noon coach to Springfield. It was scheduled to pull out as Justice Durram's trial got started.

Due to the weight of local interest and number of defendants, the hotel's dining room was customarily requisitioned as a courthouse. Gabriel Bonnet had his hired thugs to face-off friends of the ranchers, but fearing trouble, the sheriff decided that all guns were to be surrendered by anyone entering the hotel.

Before proceedings commenced, Justice Durram asked to see Maitland Crewes in private.

'How many can your jail take, Marshal?' he enquired.

Crewes thought Durram might have something else on his mind, so he answered quickly. 'Six, sir. Ten if I'm pushed, twelve if it's a Saturday night.'

'Hmm, is that Jack Ridge's estimate, or yours?'

'No, it ain't Jack's. He said to tell you twenty, if you asked.'

Durram thought for a moment, then, looked curiously amused. 'So, how many have you got cookin' in there at the moment?'

'That'll be the ten, sir.'

'Thank you, Marshal. That's all I need to know this moment.'

Mole Painter was the first to take the stand. He gave a tense, but straightforward outline of the difficulties he'd had in gaining water for his cattle. Then, within half an hour, ten other defendants had delivered brief, but moving stories of starving and thirsty herds.

It was in the almost unheard of territory of late afternoon before Justice Durram could rap for order. He frowned at the prisoners, cleared his throat and drummed his plump fingers. 'Accordin' to state law, the powers are invested in me to determine punishment at this sittin',' he began sententiously. 'Therefore, and due to the seriousness of the charge, I'm not goin' to impose the minimum sentence of a black-look wiggin' from me, an' a kick up the backside from Jack Ridge.' The judge looked across the makeshift courtroom. 'Oh no, you're gettin' *more than that*, my friends. Now, stand to hear the verdict.'

The defendants shuffled uncertainly to their feet, and Justice Durram flicked his gaze across their troubled faces. 'You all got six months in jail, or a one-thousand dollar fine. If there's any fuss, it's both. An' believe me, *that* ain't goin' to raise an eyebrow in Jefferson

City or Washington.'

Protestations and curses mingled with immediate jeering from the Bonnet camp. Jack was shocked, although he didn't show it.

'What the hell world's he livin' in? Olland murmured in Jack's ear. 'He might as well bang 'em up for life.'

Justice Durram hammered for order, and Jack and his deputy shouted for quiet.

Durram pushed a chunky law book to one side, and addressed the ranch men. 'I know there's none o' you able to raise anythin' like that amount, an' as the jail can't take on that sort o' lodgin', I have no alternative but to suspend the sentence. You're all bound over for six months, an' that means if you so much as break wind, I'll see you breakin' rocks.'

It took a moment for Durram's finding to sink in, then a soft cheer rolled through the courtroom. The dam had been freed along with the men who'd actioned it.

Jack returned to his office, and Radford Cayne called by and invited him to the ranch. 'It's none o' my business, Jack, but I'm not happy the way things have panned out between you an' young Nancy. It don't create a homely atmosphere. The girl's obviously sorry for some o' the things she's said, so why don't you try an' mend a fence or two? I'll make myself scarce if you come over.

★ ★ ★

The sun had dropped behind the Ozarks when Jack dismounted at the corral of Raising Cayne. He loosed off his horse's belly strap, then walked slowly towards the ranch house.

Nancy Cayne was already waiting for him on the stoop, but he approached doubtfully because there was something lurking unsettled at the back of his mind.

'Your pa told me you were sorry for sayin' what you did. I came out 'cause I thought there could be some truth in it . . . was hopin' anyway,' he said. 'Your pa meant well by it.'

Nancy thought for a moment, then held out her hand and gave a brief smile. 'It's true, I am sorry. I really didn't mean it.'

'I guess it's a time for us all to be regrettin' the things we said. If it weren't for what I said, Onslow Stern might be alive now.'

'An' wouldn't all of us be a lot wiser an' cleverer with the advantage of hindsight?' Nancy returned.

The two of them exchanged misgivings, mended the fences for a while, and Jack thought his prospects weren't over after all.

Jack, although mannerly and attentive, was distracted at supper. It was something that ran on from just talking about Stern. There was something at the back of his mind, and it made him uneasy and wanting to be away.

★　★　★

It was late when he left the Caynes' spread. He'd stayed longer than he meant, because of the excellence of Nancy's cooking. There was nothing immediately pressing, except the problem on his mind. It was two in the morning when it came to him. It was the documents that Harry and Onslow Stern had stolen from Lincoln Waittes. 'Important' was what Stern had said they were, and Jack had more or less forgot them.

Jack turned his horse into the livery stable, then went straight to his office where Crick Olland was sound asleep in the bunk room. He lit the lamp and pulled the packet of papers from his desk drawer. At first it didn't make any sense, but on a second scan, it came clearer. It was Lincoln Waittes's record of the alliance, an explicit diary of the group's affairs. One of the names that was clearly evident was Nancy's brother Harvey.

Engrossed with more hopeful thoughts, Jack stared into the flickering desk lamp.

The papers were a damning piece of evidence and, with an unbiased jury and a decent attorney, sufficient to make a conviction. Waittes must have guessed what Stern was going to do with such detailed and seditious papers, and Jack thought it strange there'd been no obvious attempt to retrieve them, especially as some of the dates coincided with Sunbird losing yearlings. Nonetheless, with Willard Sheet's written confession that Justice Durram was holding, Jack now had what he wanted. With returning confidence, he locked the papers back in his desk.

His eyes pricked with tiredness. Everything could wait a few hours. 'Too much sleep's a burden', his pa had once said. 'So, nothin' much stacked against me tomorrow then,' Jack muttered as he stretched himself on the office cot. As he drifted into sleep, the upshot went through his head. Arresting Gabriel Bonnet with a murder charge facing him should be no more of a chore than shuckin' peas.

14

A few hours later, Jack obtained the warrant for Bonnet's arrest, and with Crewes and Olland, he walked into the Cooncan House Saloon.

Knowing that Bonnet kept late hours, he reckoned on the saloon owner still being in his bed. The only person about was the potboy indolently brooming up the night's mess, and Jack asked him where Bonnet was.

'Mr Bonnet said not to tell anyone where he was, if he weren't here. An' he ain't here.'

'I'm the sheriff. You can tell me.'

'No. He mentioned you in particular.'

And that was all Jack got out of him. The door to Bonnet's office opened and a mixed-blood whom Jack recognized as Crespo Chance stood there defiantly.

The man's eyes were dark, his

features inscrutable. He was new in town, a mercenary gunman of whom Jack had learned from the county circulars.

'The boy's just gone an' told you. Mr Bonnet's not here.' The gunman sniffed superciliously. 'What do you want him for?'

Jack shot a glance at his deputy, then, pushing the man to one side, he stepped quickly through the door. But the gunman and the boy were right. Bonnet wasn't there. His bed in the through-room of his office had only been used by Chance.

'If there's a next time, remember this,' the gunman said, and smiled malevolently as he bade Jack farewell.

Jack saddled his horse at the livery stable then rode back to Raising Cayne. He rode fast to the ranch house and both Cayne and Nancy stepped out to meet him. He hadn't meant to reveal his true feelings or plans, but with Harvey involved he felt it was incumbent on the sheriff's office to give

Cayne a fuller picture.

Cayne's face remained calm, but pained. 'This don't come as a total surprise, Jack, an' I'm not one for askin' favours. But could you consider givin' the boy a chance to square himself? Whatever you've got on him, it can't be irrevocable. If your law's goin' to be lenient, maybe you can lean a tad the other way.'

The sheriff had reckoned on Cayne's appeal, but he was resolute. 'He'll have the right to a defence, Mr Cayne, the same as anyone else. He'll be brought to trial, an' a jury can decide to be lenient or not, not you or me.'

There was an uneasy silence, and Jack knew he'd said too much, thought that maybe he should have kept his mouth shut. Now, Cayne would prob- ably warn off his son.

'Where is this *evidence* you have?' Nancy asked eventually.

Jack looked at her sharply. 'A jury will meet for a special session. That's where it's goin' to be,' he said.

Nancy's eyes were very cool blue now, Jack noticed, as he saw them flick towards a partly closed door that led off the main room.

Jack didn't spare his horse too much as he raced back to town. He was angry and distrustful, knew he had good right, when he saw a lone horseman cutting across the north range of Raising Cayne.

He hitched his sweating horse to the rail and walked into his office. His deputy turned in his chair and looked up surprised, grabbed an open newsheet from the desk. 'Kept this for you, Jack. Look here,' he said, enthusiastically holding up a copy of the *Eldon Bugle*.

Jack read an inside page of the newspaper. Tayler Gemson out of Deepwater County had been appointed Deputy United States Marshal. In an interview, the new Deputy of Eldon was reported to be instigating an immediate and rigorous campaign to clean up the territory. According to Gemson, time had run out for lawlessness and outlawry north of the Ozark Lakes. Among those on a wanted list was Harry Ridge.

Jack laughed. 'I wouldn't have believed this if I hadn't read it with my own eyes,' he said. 'I wonder if they got the news out where Harry's hidin'?' He tore the clipping, folded it and shoved it under his hat. 'Has Bonnet come back?'

Olland shook his head 'Nope. My money says he'll be celebratin'. Maybe on one o' them big trout ponds with Gemson.'

With no pressing law business, Jack decided to do something else just as worthwhile and ride out to the ranch to see Seth Carlisle. But, as he pulled out of the livery stable, he met him. He was with Max Swilley in the prospector's wagon carrying supplies.

'Just my luck. I was on the way out to Sunbird,' he said, looping his horse to the back stay. He tucked himself comfortably between two sacks of oats and brought the two of them up to date, handed over the news clipping to Max.

★ ★ ★

It was full dark when the wagon topped the low, five mile bluff. 'Someone's at home,' Seth said, when they saw lights flickering in Sunbird's ranch house.

Max reined-in the wagon mule and glanced sideways at Jack. 'Harry wouldn't be puttin' a match to goddamn party lanterns.'

Jack peered through the darkness. 'Looks like three horses. I reckon I know who they are, an' what they want, an' they ain't friendlies.'

Max and Seth dropped from their seats and Jack rolled from the back of the wagon. Max pulled out Stern's big Martini-Henry and Seth checked his Colt. The three men looked at each tother then walked steadily on to the ranch house. Jack and Seth approached the front entrance, and Max moved around the side.

Max was away from any light when he stumbled into an up-ended feed trough. The stock of his long gun banged against the metal, and within seconds a shotgun blasted out from a front window. It was followed immediately by a hail of gunfire pouring from all the ranch-house windows.

The night was lit by yellow flashes as Jack yelled. 'You picked the wrong place this time. You're on my property, an' you ain't got many choices about what to do.' He knew the threat of a fire-powered assault was an empty one. It was arguably his own house he'd be breaking up.

The men inside were obviously thinking the same thing, and a scornful yell and more bullets stormed around Jack and Seth.

Jack beckoned. 'Can you keep 'em busy while I get round the back?' he asked.

Seth looked calmly at the sheriff. 'I don't think I can, Jack. Not when it's my turn to get more involved. *I'll* go up through the storm-trap; *you* look out for Max. Won't be more'n three minutes.' And he moved away before Jack could stop him.

Max had been crouching in the dark. 'What's Seth up to?' he called quietly as he approached Jack who was standing calmly in deep shadow. Now there was only sporadic fire from the windows. It seemed the men inside had decided not to waste their ammunition.

Jack held up his hand to indicate that Max should hold up. He listened to the spooked horses at the hitching rail as they continued to stamp and snort at the clamour. Then from inside the ranch house, he heard the sharp noise of the Navy Colt. There were two shots in rapid succession followed by an agonized yell. There was a moment of silence before Seth called out for him and Max.

With guns drawn and thrust forward, the two men came loping into the room. Max remained in the doorway and Jack quickly edged around the side wall. One man was crumpled by the window. He was gripping a Colt but quickly dying. Amos Heron sat propped against the leg of a table. His face was rigid from the wound deep in his shoulder, and blood oozed across his vest. Standing in the middle of the room was the man Jack expected to see. Harvey Cayne's face was twisted with rage and his fists were clenched tight.

Jack muttered an oath, looked hard at Seth and recalled what Stern had discovered about his prowess with guns. Then he stepped across to Cayne and with the back of his hand whipped a savage smack across his face. 'This is all down to you, you little grub,' he snarled. 'This is my house an' I know what you're doin' here.'

Max cut in. 'We'd better take Amos into town, Jack, he's losin' his liquor,' he said.

'Not yet.'

Cayne's face was quickly draining of colour and his eyes were shifting from one face to another. 'You can all go to hell,' he swore, his pig-headedness and vocabulary reminding Jack of Willard Sheet.

Then, and unexpectedly, Cayne's foot swung up, and the toe of his boot caught Jack in the groin. Jack grunted and doubled back in pain, and both men went crashing into Seth. Cayne snatched at Jack's holster, and then staggered sideways. His thumb clawed back the hammer of the pistol, and he levelled it at Jack's chest.

There was one great blast of a shot from the doorway and a thick coil of smoke rose from Max's rifle. The impact of the big calibre bullet took Harvey Cayne off his feet and he was dead long before he hit the far wall.

Max turned the barrel of the gun towards the floor. 'Christ, Jack, I didn't mean . . . '

Jack stooped, winced painfully as he picked up his gun from Cayne's lifeless fingers. 'I'd like to think you *did*, Max,' he seethed. 'Otherwise it would be *me* lyin' here.'

Max looked towards Seth. 'I didn't mean to *kill* him.'

'That gun don't do much else, Max.' Seth took the rifle from Max's grasp. 'An' you probably just saved more'n one life.'

'He wasn't warned off by his pa,' Jack said almost absent-mindedly, as he stared down at Cayne's body. 'He'd been at the ranch. He was listenin' when I told his sister an' his pa that I'd got evidence. He probably told Bonnet.' Jack looked to Amos Heron. 'Is that right?' he asked him. 'What were you lookin' for?'

'Papers. Some sort o' papers. I'm hurtin' real bad, Sheriff,' Heron replied, his strength and interest failing.

'I guess Radford Cayne will be real proud o' you,' Jack muttered with disgust.

Max turned suddenly and looked into the night. 'Somebody comin',' he said.

Jack nodded knowingly. 'Yeah, that'll be Crick, come to say that Bonnet's returned. Max, can you and Seth load Heron onto his horse? I don't want to touch him.'

Crick Olland dropped his horse's reins and ran up the steps at the front of the ranch house. He came through the door and looked around him. His jaw dropped, and his eyes rolled around before resting on the bloody mess of Harvey Cayne.

'Later,' Jack said, his short answer to any question from his deputy.

Heron was lifted onto his horse, and Cayne was laid in the wagon with his horse hitched on behind. The riders moved south back towards the long bluff.

As they came onto Raising Cayne land, Olland left them and headed for town with Amos Heron. Jack advised Max to go back to Sunbird while he rode on with Seth.

Jack dismounted and stepped up to the ranch house. He hesitated, then rapped purposefully at the door. Nancy opened it, looked aloof and moved away as her father arrived. Cayne folded a pair of reading glasses and slotted them into a waistcoat pocket. In the light from the porch lamps he could see Seth and the prospector's wagon, but not the body of his son below the panels.

'I think we should step inside,' Jack said moving forward. He closed the door quietly after him, a euphemism to someway cushion the blow. 'It's Harvey, Mr Cayne,' he started.

But Radford Cayne had already figured out some of what was happening. 'I guess we all had it comin'. Badly wounded, is he?' he asked simply.

Jack shook his head. 'Not this time. He's dead, Mr Cayne.'

Cayne's hand clutched at the door frame for support. He uttered a low guttural gasp, and his shoulders sagged. Then he stiffened, took a step towards the door and Jack opened it. Cayne pushed him to one side, and looked out at Seth.

'Bring him in.' Cayne's torment

made his words hardly audible.

Nancy came to the corner of the front landing and looked intently at the wagon. But she didn't watch as Jack and Seth carried Harvey's blood-spattered body into the house and rested him across a sofa.

'How'd this happen?' Cayne asked forlornly.

Jack sensed that Nancy was now in the doorway looking at him, but he wasn't going to turn and meet her eyes.

'He was goin' to shoot me, with my own gun in my own home. If he'd done that, he would have had to shoot Max an' Seth. Someone had to stop him.' Jack told the rest fast and straight with no tempering frills. The best defence is a good offence. That was another military gambit from the classroom — one that Jack could try hiding behind expediently. 'He won't be standin' trial, Mr Cayne. An' I'll think about holdin' back parts o' the evidence. It ain't no matter to anyone,' he offered.

* * *

Half an hour after they'd ridden out, Jack turned to Seth and ran through some thoughts. 'Someone got Harvey to do the risky work,' he said, 'but his family's responsible for his death.'

'Yeah, both of 'em,' Seth replied.

'Can't help thinkin' that I might be partly to blame, though.'

'How'd you reckon that?' Seth asked.

'Well, if I hadn't gone out there to tell 'em about that goddamn evidence, he wouldn't have known.'

'His pa would have told him. Anyways, they could've stopped him. There's nothin' for you to peg yourself up on.'

'We'll need Max,' Jack said after riding for another hour 'There'll be an inquest in the mornin'.'

* * *

Olland had been waiting for Jack to reach town, and together they wasted no time in getting to the Cooncan. They were determined and looked like the onset of trouble. Even one or two suspecting townsfolk failed to acknowledge them.

Maitland Crewes was already there, and with Olland they covered the room. Jack walked straight across to Bonnet's door and knocked loudly, took a step back as the door swung open.

'You got good reason for this?' Holding a short-barrelled Colt close to his side, Bonnet looked dangerous as he stood framed in the backlight.

Jack stood motionless. 'Good enough,' he said. 'I've come to warn you . . . advise you, that you're under arrest.'

Bonnet considered Jack's ultimatum for a moment. 'Well, you advised me. Is that all?' he asked with something like a sneer crossing his face.

'No, not quite. If you so much as flinch while you're holdin' that sidearm, my deputy's got shoot-to-kill orders.'

Bonnet's eyes flicked from the sheriff out to the saloon, but he made no move. Having seen the look on Jack's face, he knew he hadn't been given options. 'What's the charge?' he asked.

'Murder, or somethin' close. There'll be a label for it, so don't go makin' a fuss. I'll force a bracelet round your goddamn neck if I have to.'

'So who'm I supposed to have murdered, Ridge?'

Jack didn't bother to answer. 'Just drop the gun, or you won't be livin' to find out.'

As Bonnet loosed his fingers, Crewes's voice boomed across the saloon. 'Don't move. Put your hands flat on the bar.'

The marshal had seen a movement from the barman. The man was uncertain of his standpoint and looked to Bonnet for some sign of allegiance.

'Go an' see Waittes. Tell him to get bail money,' the saloon owner said, and smiled grimly.

15

The news that Gabriel Bonnet had been arrested spread fast. The decent, law-abiding citizens backed the sheriff, but the jury was crammed with those influenced by, and friendly towards both Bonnet and Lincoln Waittes. Even the prosecuting attorney was a man whose allegiance was fingered by the banker. Bonnet attempted to get bail, but the honourable Justice Durram wouldn't offer anything other than the assurance of a speedy trial.

There was also Harvey Cayne's death to deal with, and when the inquest was opened at Raising Cayne Ranch the following morning, the men who flanked the alliance were there.

Jack told his story and Max Swilley, Seth Carlisle and Crick Olland followed. Halfway through testimony, Crespo Chance noisily claimed a verdict be brought against Max. But, ever mindful of Jack's assurance that he'd bury any adverse evidence against his son, Radford Cayne was there to help the Sunbird man in acquittal.

When the crowd had left, Jack rode to Sunbird to have a talk with his old friend Seth. Jack was troubled by Harry. When his brother heard of Gemson's new appointment as deputy marshal, he might take affairs into his own hands. Detaining Bonnet might be a short-lived concern.

Seth gave Jack his opinion. 'They're movin' into a corner, an' Waittes ain't goin' to sit idly by. They'll take it to Springfield, an' Durram will have to set bail.' He gave Jack a wily look. 'Bonnet'll get out, as sure as eggs is eggs. Then they'll string the case along for months. So maybe Harry's methods of *makin' battle with 'em* really are worth considerin'.'

★　★　★

Jack was mulling over rational options as he returned to Comeback. The late sun had finally slid away and there was no sound other than his horse's hoofs and a testy snort. He was drowsy, his chin bobbling against his chest, when a hammer blow caught him hard in the side of his head. He heard a distant crack as he slipped gently forward trying to grip himself in the saddle. He toppled, the sweat, hot and strong as the side of his face crushed down the horse's withers. The ground flashed pale colours, then dark shadows as it met his fall.

He came up from the blackness and the pain immediately made him sick. He shivered and raised a hand to his tacky, matted hair. He rolled onto his side and vomited again, held the sides of his head between his fingers. He groaned for a few minutes then, with his head hanging down, he eased himself on to his knees. From somewhere near, a snort eddied through the air, and Jack gave a thin tortured whistle. He heard the clink of his horse's hoofs as it moved in close, and he reached out for a stirrup. Cursing, and taking quick, shallow breaths, he dragged himself up and into the saddle. Clutching the reins in one hand and a hank of mane in the other, he told the horse to start walking.

On the deliberate wander to the outskirts of town, the pain gradually cleared. His hat was gone and the night air blew coolly against his forehead. By the time they reached the livery stable he was suffering from a sharp but tolerable throb. 'No worse'n a big brother's backhand,' he murmured and tested a minor smile.

He called in on Doc Pagham and had his wound dressed. 'You're lucky. A little to the side, and you'd be lookin' for an assignment in blind town,' the doc had said.

Jack had just worked out what the doc had meant, when Olland came in with his concern and questions about his appearance. But Jack wanted an explanation about Bonnet's release.

'They got a high-priced lawyer up from Springfield,' Olland began. 'He threatened a change o' venue. Justice Durram said it was a point o' law, an' he had to set bail.'

'Goddamnit, I'd'a ruled on point o' law all right . . . my boot pointed right up his ass. What time was this . . . that he got out?'

The deputy shrugged. 'I'm not certain, Jack. Must've been early this afternoon.'

'That could account for the near bullet in my brain.'

'I don't suppose you saw anythin'?'

Jack shook his head slowly. 'No. I was actually half asleep . . . not too much on the lookout. Whoever it was must've thought they'd put me in the sandhills.'

The deputy nodded thoughtfully. 'There's talk o' you goin' before the jury in the mornin' to give evidence against Waittes. You reckon the two are connected?'

Jack gave a small smile. 'Yeah, reckon.

It would be a good new twist if they could sentence him without hearin' it.'

'An' maybe you'd live a while longer,' Olland muttered.

They had a meal at the hotel, then Jack wondered what the response would be if he poked his nose into the Cooncan. It didn't take long to find out. They'd hardly set foot inside, when Gabriel Bonnet came straight at them. But if he was surprised at seeing Jack, he made good use of his professional poker face.

'Whatever trouble you been in, Sheriff, I hope you ain't come over here to sort it out,' he said. 'I don't reckon me or my business can take much more o' your sort o' law. By the look o' you, someone else has been thinkin' the same.'

'One day you'll have to tell me what sort o' law you do want,' Jack answered.

An offhand smirk was Bonnet's only response, although on the way back to his office he spoke briefly to Crespo Chance.

'He talks like he ain't even suspected,' Olland said.

'Yeah, I know. But somethin's happenin', I just know it. Let's wait awhile.'

The two lawmen had nearly finished their drinks when Max Swilley pushed hurriedly through the doors of the saloon. 'Harry's got his horns lowered,' he said breathlessly. 'When I told him Gemson was a marshal, he said 'not for long', an' dug spurs. There's one unlucky lawman who ain't goin' to work his time, Jack.'

No sooner had the men moved away from the bar, than Lincoln Waittes duly arrived.

'You're right, Jack. Looks like things're gettin' interestin' hereabouts,' Olland agreed.

As Waittes stood in silent surprise, a look of complicity dragged at his face. It was what Jack had been expecting to see earlier from Bonnet.

The banker was suddenly fearful, and for good reason. The evidence he was going to use to pressure his colleagues had rebounded. Bonnet had got wind, and he had arrived to make his excuses.

Jack, Max and Olland each gave the banker an indifferent look, then went straight to the sheriff's office.

'How the hell do we stop Harry?' Jack asked, as he kicked the door shut.

'I can't say *how*, but I know *who*,' Olland responded. 'Your brother's goin' straight for Gemson, an' he ain't goin' to raise his hands to the likes o' me.'

Jack eyed his deputy and nodded, accepted the reasoning. 'OK. You ride to Cole Camp, Max. I'll go to Eldon,' he said. 'Gemson could be at either. If you find him, dog him. But keep your eyes wide open. He might know some real shady places.'

Jack gathered the packet of papers from his desk. Seth told him it would be a waste of time to present the evidence to a jury, but Jack was adamant and spent nearly an hour discussing it with Justice Durram. The next morning he turned the evidence over to court and waited. It was all he could do. If the jury indicted the three men, it might be possible to reach Harry and stop him shooting Tayler Gemson.

There was no doubt about the hearing being a contentious and unruly session. Voices were raised in fiery disputes for most of the day. As soon as dark came, meals were brought in while Jack sat fiddling in the office, or patrolling Main Street. If Harry did kill Gemson, he'd have to do something. The clash on the timberline was work, a gnat's nip in comparison to a brothers' fight.

Jack was carving the shape of a lone star into a desk panel with a penknife, when Crick Olland came in and sat down.

'They're done arguin',' he reported wearily. Then he allowed a small smile to move the corners of his mouth. 'An' they're indicted. All goddamn three of 'em.'

Jack got up from his chair, pounded his fist against his leg. Then he found himself a hat and beat it around a bit.

'You goin' to arrest 'em?' Maitland Crewes wanted to know immediately.

Jack tugged at the headband of the hat until it eased its shape. 'No, not yet,' he said. 'They know my reach. We'll arrest 'em when I get back. I've got to find Harry before he finds Gemson.

★ ★ ★

In the deep night-time silence that brimmed the range, Radford Cayne heard him arrive. The light spilled onto the broad veranda when Cayne opened the front door to meet him, but he made no move to invite Jack inside.

With no preliminaries, Jack told of the outcome of the hearing, and when he'd done, it was Nancy who stepped out to confront him.

'So you'll be riding after your brother then?' she asked with a curious lack of feeling or interest in her voice.

Jack could understand how Nancy would feel about the death of Harvey, but not the way she acted towards him personally. 'You must have some weird reason to act like this,' he exclaimed. 'I'm tryin' to prevent another killin' goddamnit . . . maybe *Harry's*. An' in case you weren't aware of it, so far he's actually *innocent*.'

He shook his head at her sadly and, in frustration, he thumped his spurs. He was gone too fast and too soon to see the tear, the way she grasped her father's hand.

16

It wasn't until the lights of Raising Cayne had long faded from sight, that Jack noticed the flying specks of foam, then the gleam of sweat that covered his horse's neck. He eased to a trot, slapped a hand against the wet hair. 'No need to take it out on you,' he said.

On the second night he tied his horse to a rail in front of the Bullhead Saloon in Eldon. The town was notorious in and around the fingers of the Ozark Lakes. Jack knew that if Harry had been there, some other man would know it.

All kinds of cigarette, cigar and pipe smoke billowed among the low rafters of the drinking and gambling room. Jack had removed his badge, but his watchful eye took in most of the customers as he walked slowly to the bar.

He recognized two men as former

workers of Gabriel Bonnet, but there was no sign of Harry, or Gemson. The bartender looked to Jack for his drink.

Jack shook his head. 'It's the boss I want,' he said.

The bartender made a short, jerky movement with his chin. Almost in the same instant Jack knew there was somebody standing close behind him, and he smiled at the move. He turned and stood eye to eye with a tall, thin Chinaman.

The saloon owner bowed ever so slightly to the sheriff. 'My name's Robert Lee, and I own this establishment. We don't all wash shirts, if that's what you're thinkin'.'

'It isn't,' Jack returned. 'I'm wonderin' where the hell it was you just come from. You got somewhere we could talk?'

The saloon owner raised an eyebrow, then looked around him confidently. He nodded, and led Jack to one of two curtained-off, adjoining booths.

Jack explained his problem and Lee shook his head. 'I know nothing of the first man you speak of. But the other one's our new deputy. He was in, maybe three days ago. Perhaps you'd like a drink, Sheriff? You've some riding ahead of you.' Lee gave a deadpan, gold-toothed grin.

'I would, but I'm not goin' to. I think you've told me what I wanted to know.'

Lee wouldn't or couldn't say any more, and Jack couldn't read which. He nodded his appreciation and thanked the man, then made his way out of the saloon. If Gemson was more than a day ahead of him, it was a hopeless chase. He would have to take a chance on Max Swilley catching up with Harry.

Within an hour Jack was on the trail to Comeback. And Gabriel Bonnet and Lincoln Waittes were about to go through the turmoil and displeasure of Jack putting some law into place.

★ ★ ★

The moment he was sure Jack had left his saloon, Robert Lee entered the second booth. Sitting at a card table with his hand wrapped around the cylinder of a Colt was Tayler Gemson, and he laughed loudly.

'Waittes an' Bonnet both indicted? Well, ain't that a durn shame. You know, I always had a feelin' about bankers, Robert Lee. It ain't really a profession for honest men,' he chortled. 'Still, well done. Our first bit o' mutual business, an' well-handled.'

The Chinaman shrugged. 'I don't think so. I believe you and your friends are in real trouble.'

Gemson's laughing continued. 'Naagh. I'm a US deputy marshal. Neither o' the Ridges can touch me. Nobody can.'

Robert Lee contemplated Gemson's assertion. 'If the man who's just left here is one of the men you're up against, they'll do a lot more than just *touch* you,' he said after a long moment.

The one-time sheriff of Comeback

elbowed his way through the crowded saloon and into the street. He was after an advantage, and right now didn't care for the whereabouts of Harry Ridge, or for Robert Lee's warning. He saw no reason why he couldn't return to Comeback, other than the truism of nobody much ever did. Once on the driver's plate, he'd be difficult to get down, and Jack Ridge would be forced to safeguard him. Gemson's reverie was so pleasing that he failed to see the rider who'd followed him out of town, started to track him north-west from Eldon.

★ ★ ★

It was two in the morning when Gemson neared one of Raising Cayne's outermost line shacks. It was unoccupied and he decided to spend the rest of the night there. He had intended to meet with his new boss, Orville Grate, in Eldon, but Grate was an old timer and would know enough to follow him to Comeback.

As dawn streaked across the big Missouri sky, Gemson stretched and poked around the line shack's staple provisions. He walked outside with a hot cup of coffee, held up short when a quiet voice surprised him. The tin mug fell from his fingers, spilled down his front and across his boots as the container clanked onto the rocky-strewn ground.

Harry was unmoving. His hands were at his sides and he was very unsmiling. His voice was unemotional and it drained life from the marshal's face.

'The new US deputy marshal's goin' to get another mention in the *Eldon Bugle*. But this time, Gemson, it's in the obituary column,' he suggested acidly.

'You ain't a murderer, Ridge,' Gemson said, trying to gain some composure. 'We both know that.'

'I'm glad to hear it, Gemson. Now you try an' remember who killed my father, an' I won't make us both into liars.'

Harry stepped into the cabin. In a moment he came back out with another tin mug and the marshal's gunbelt over his shoulder. He laid the gunbelt at his feet, and while he finger-tested the temperature of the scalding coffee, his eyes never moved from Gemson's face.

'If this brew ain't to my likin', Gemson, I'm goin' to pour it where your spillin' just missed,' he threatened.

Gemson swayed backwards. 'I weren't after you. I've been accused alongside Waittes an' Bonnet. It looks best if I give myself up, so I'm goin' back.'

A cruel twitch moved in Harry's face, and he tossed Gemson his gunbelt. 'Tell me what happened to my pa, while you put this on.'

Gemson swallowed hard and tried again. 'Harvey Cayne hired Hawker Bream to shoot your pa, an' that's the God's honest truth. Max Swilley blew young Cayne apart, an' you did for Bream.'

'But Bream used an old Spencer re-bore. *Your* Spencer re-bore, Gemson. The one you got there in the shack. Tell a lie when the truth don't fit, eh?' Harry bit out the words sourly. 'It took three o' you to shoot him down.' Harry moved his coat away from his side, revealed one of his father's matched .44 revolvers.

Gemson knew that his time had run out, and leaned to fasten the holster strap to his leg. But Harry knew it was a pointless deception as Gemson flung himself to one side and drew his Colt. With his finger on the trigger, he flip-cocked the hammer twice, then three times in short rapid succession. As he hit the ground heavily he was watching Harry, but there was confusion in his eyes as he doubled from the waist. He rolled into a ball and grimaced as he tasted his own blood. He tried to keep his eyes open, but they clouded. He rasped out the words, strangely worried that Harry wouldn't hear. 'Pay the goddamn ferryman.'

'There'll be no goddamn charge for you,' Harry rasped. Then he whistled for his horse and still clutching his revolver he climbed into the saddle. Looking down at Gemson's body, he sat thinking for a few seconds. 'That makes four of 'em now, Pa,' he said.

It must have been his sixth sense that made Harry dip forward then. A bullet smashed into the broken shale, and he heard the echo of the rifle shot. He cursed and kicked at the horse's flanks with his spurs as another bullet exploded into the ground close by. He bent low over the animal's neck, and with a contemptuous shout swerved away to the nearest tract of timberline.

⋆　⋆　⋆

Six hours later, Harry was slowly walking his horse. He was in the timberline, slanting back and forth on the passable side of the Mossbank, when another horse whinnied somewhere behind him. He straightened in the saddle and swung up his Winchester as two close-together shots came ripping out of stand of pine almost fifty yards away.

With a streak of numbing pain, he was hit in his right side, and he almost pitched from the saddle. 'Jeeesus, who the hell are you?' he yelled, while managing a single returning shot. The rifle blasted again, and the next bullet thudded into his thigh and the horse reared. It snorted wildly before going down, taking Harry with it. Half stunned and unable to move, he heard a man's voice call out, and then a horse moved up and away through the dense timber before the blackness took him.

17

Jack reached town in the early morning, but it was mid afternoon before Olland's voice woke him. Max Swilley was also in the office when he emerged from his bunk room.

'Did you find Harry?' Max asked.

Jack yawned, and shook his head. 'No one's seen him. An' you always got to believe what a Chinamen tells you.'

Max returned a confused look. 'I couldn't find out much either. Nobody's seen 'em.'

'Maybe I was right. Maybe they're teamed up, an' gone fishin' after all,' Olland said.

Jack turned to his deputy. 'Get hold o' Crewes. We'll get them warrants out.'

'I don't think we will, Jack,' Olland offered somewhat awkwardly. 'Waittes an' Bonnet gave 'emselves up. But there was some sort o' wrong doin', an' there's no charges bein' brought. Wakin' you up to tell you, wouldn't have helped.'

Jack's fist clenched. 'What sort o' wrong doin'?'

Olland shrugged. 'Ain't my line of work.'

'Anythin' else I should know about?' Jack asked grimly.

'Well, Waittes an' Bonnet are pretty snorty with each other. Waittes has got loan foreclosures on all the spreads that owe money. Justice Durram says it's legal. He said that if any o' the ranchers had hired attorneys, they'd have saved 'emselves all this trouble.'

Jack shook his head frustratedly, then pointed a finger at his deputy. 'I blame you for all this, Crick,' he said.

Olland looked mystified. 'Why? Why the hell me?'

'It's delegation . . . one o' the benefits o' bein' sheriff,' Jack told him. 'Apart from the fact I can't think of anythin' else to do right now,' he continued quickly. 'Times sure change.

I mean, who the hell ever hired an attorney to let 'em heave cows. The only thing that ever got hired out here's a puddin' foot mare or a hay wagon. Them ranchers ain't gettin' anywhere, as long as the likes o' Waittes an' Bonnet are undercuttin' their word an' their hard work.'

'But Waittes is runnin' scared now. He's even asked Bonnet to loan him a couple o' men with guns. Sounds like he's gettin' real lynchy.'

'Huh, we'll see about that,' Jack said, and was straightaway off to the banker's home.

'I hope you're here to tell me about my protection, Sheriff,' Waittes said anxiously.

'Yeah, that's about it, Mr Waittes. As sheriff I ain't got much choice,' Jack accepted. 'But I'm also warnin' you that if you hire anyone outside o' the law, I'll see you behind bars. At least that'll keep you safe. Anyway, I heard the Devil protects his own,' he added, sharply as he turned away.

The banker was so taken aback at Jack's ultimatum, that he made no response other than an incredulous gape.

Jack went back to his office and told Olland and Maitland Crewes to arrange the banker's protection. Then he got a horse from the livery stable and rode out to try and quell any trouble before it reached town. His first call was at the ranch of a very dogged Mole Painter.

'We ain't waitin' for the law this time, Sheriff. So don't go gettin' in the way. We got us a pair o' pigs to poke,' was the intolerant response.

As he turned away, Jack shouted to the old rancher, 'Just remember, you didn't wait for the law last time, Mole.'

Hamilton Sugget's anger was just as great. Jack's argument was just as ineffective, and he couldn't blame them for feeling the way they did. But he was an appointed sheriff, and would only let them get to Waittes through his badge. 'I never told Mole, but I'm tellin' you, Ham,' he said. 'Most o' you are still bound over. If Gregor Poe gets wind o' your intentions ... well, I wouldn't want to go upsettin' that peptic ol' son-of-a-bitch.'

★ ★ ★

Jack didn't waste any time in his search for deputies. The few hands who were available weren't having anything to do with protecting Lincoln Waittes. As a last resort, he tried Gabriel Bonnet. He'd been a collaborator with Waittes, but Jack couldn't believe the saloon owner would support any underdog in the forming of a vigilante group.

Bonnet was mockingly friendly as Jack followed him into his office. 'So you'd like to raise a picket around the Lincoln Waittes house, eh? Hmm. I'm guessin' you had no luck elsewhere.'

Jack nodded. 'It ain't a question of me likin' to raise anythin'. It's a lawful duty, an' I'm down to Olland an' Crewes.'

'Give me one good reason why I

should help you, Sheriff?' Bonnet asked.

Jack placed the toe of his boot on the seat of Bonnet's snug chair. 'Waittes has got your name in a diary that lists just about all them wrong doin's o' yours. If any lynch mob gets to him, he'll go down singin' 'cause that's the sort o' man he is. How about that, Gabriel? Can you afford to risk it?'

Bonnet sniffed nonchalantly and indicated the office door. 'Yeah, well, when you put it like that Sheriff. I'll get together a few men, I might even be there myself.'

After collecting ammunition and a rifle, Jack went to see the banker again. Sophie let him in, and Jack told them what he'd arranged with Bonnet.

Waittes was clearly scared. 'Bonnet will kill me,' he said.

Jack shook his head. 'No, that's what you're supposed to think, Mr Waittes. But you're worth a hell of a lot more alive.'

Knuckles rapped against the front

door and before Jack could stop her, Sophie had opened it. He stood behind her, his hand on his gun. It was Bonnet. He took off his hat and Jack followed him through into the study.

'Good evenin', Lincoln,' the saloon owner said. 'I suppose the sheriff has told you, I've brought men who've been delegated to protect you.'

Before Waittes could respond, there was a sudden shouting from the street and Jack stepped out onto the porch. Bonnet's motley collection of bar-tender, croupier and a few others were stationed around the house. Jack saw Crick Olland talking to Hamilton Sugget across the street and Crewes was close beside him. With Sugget, shoulder-to-shoulder between them, they approached the house.

'Well, what's it goin' to be this time, Ham?' Jack said. 'You sure don't frighten off easy.'

Sugget had retained his anger. 'I've more'n a dozen men here, Sheriff, an' I don't want anyone to get hurt. You and the girl please get out of the way. It's the banker we want.'

Jack smiled coldly. 'If you don't want anyone to get hurt, you shoulda stayed at home. Bonnet's men are already here.'

Sugget instantly felt wrong-footed and his dismayed showed. 'Bonnet's men are here? Where are they?'

'If you want to see 'em, Crick can introduce you,' Jack said, looking around him. Then he leaned in close. 'If you pursue this, I'll make sure we take out the officers first. Now, ain't that frightenin' enough to get you back home?'

The rancher knew of necessity the sheriff wasn't bluffing. There was proof that the Ridges did kill men if they had to. He backed into the street, had a knowing word with his men and in a few minutes came back. 'Powerful argument, Sheriff. An' Waittes ain't worth spillin' blood over.'

Jack looked at him, nodded and smiled wickedly. '*Yours*,' he mouthed silently.

Sugget hadn't quite finished 'Get him to cancel the foreclosures. That'll be our trade-off for the gun-fight. You tell him that.'

'I'll tell him,' Jack promised.

18

When those who'd had thoughts of lynch law had vanished from town, Bonnet sent his men back to the saloon. Jack saw his deputy and the marshal off on a circuit of the town.

'Could the sheriff take an hour off to take me for a ride?' Sophie Waittes asked.

Jack grinned. 'Yeah, you're goddamn right he could. Would that be with or without guns?'

'*I'm* not that dangerous,' she replied turning her head away. 'I think it's *those* around me.'

Jack got a rig from the livery stable and they trotted east to where the five-mile bluff overlooked a creek of the Mossbank.

'It don't look much, but there's catfish in there as big as your arm. Well, there was when we were knee-highs.'

Jack laughed, then looked more closely at Sophie. 'You don't want to hear my fishin' stories, do you?' he said.

Sophie looked quickly up at the sky, then down at her clasped hands. 'No. I want you to tell me about those men. What was going on back there? What is it that my father's involved in?'

Jack was surprised that she didn't seem to know her *father* was one of those dangerous people around her. 'I don't rightly understand what you're askin', Sophie,' he said. 'Are you sayin' you don't know what your father's been doin?'

Sophie shook her head. 'He doesn't tell me anything. Nor my mother. But you know, and I want you to tell me.'

Jack could only guess at whether Waittes was trying to protect his wife and daughter, or his own standing in their eyes. He told her what he knew. Some of it was well known, but some of it wasn't. All of it was the truth. 'That's the marrow of it, Sophie. If I can't stop Harry, he'll have a crack at your father, an' now you know why.'

It was getting late when they got back to town. As Sophie turned to get down from the rig outside her house, a man came running from the house to meet them. It was one of the bank clerks.

'I woulda sent someone out for you, but I didn't know where you'd gone.' The man's voice was rising with emotion.

Jack vaulted to the ground. 'What's happened?'

'It's Mr Waittes. He's been shot . . . dead.'

Jack cursed and reached out for Sophie as she slid down from the buggy. He helped her into the house, was confronted by the body of her father on the floor in front of them. Through a half-open door into a side room he caught sight of Waittes's wife. She was sitting stiffly in a high-back chair, staring out at him. But there was no sign of comprehension in her tearful eyes.

From the clerk, Jack got as much of

the story as he could. Jumpily, the man described how Waittes had been talking quietly with Bonnet, and then raised voices. Bonnet had started shouting and swearing at Waittes. Then the banker threatened Bonnet, before the gunshot.

The clerk had seen Bonnet heading back along the street towards his saloon. He himself had been too nervous to do much else, other than to wait in shock.

For a short moment, Jack pondered on Sophie's bleak judgement of the town and its citizens. 'Go get Olland and Crewes,' he told the clerk. 'Tell' em to bring some guns. Then find the doc, he'll know what to do, to take care of it all.'

The grief was drawing at Sophie's face, but there was also something else, something unsettled. 'You're going to find him?' she asked, looking at Jack as if she wasn't certain of his intent.

He gripped her hand and smiled grimly. 'Not on my own I ain't. But I'll get him, I promise.'

Harry Ridge's eyes were open but he saw nothing, though gradually, and sharpened by pain, awareness crept through him. He lay on the ground with one shoulder crushed against the rim of a large, lichen-covered rock. The shadows of first dark were claiming the gully, and far overhead clouds were edged with the ebbing rays of the sun.

He moved and pain streaked through him, caused fresh blood to seep under the sodden clothes along his right side. He lay still again and, as he drifted in and out of consciousness, he pondered on the identity of who'd been sent to shoot him. Then he heard soft, breathy puffing, and he turned his head. His horse was standing about fifteeen feet away, mud-caked and with a twisted saddle, it stood patiently waiting, watching him. Harry wasn't alone, and he suddenly felt more able to face up to what had happened, what to do next. Gritting his teeth against the deep hurt, he hitched himself out from the rock and pulled himself into a sitting position.

His leg was useless, his right arm numb with pain. But slowly and carefully, he worked his arms and shoulders from his coat. It took all of his reserve to remove his sodden, bloodstained shirt and rip it into two pieces. One, he wrapped around his waist above his belt to try and cover the the raw, seeping gash beneath. The other, he wrapped around his left thigh over his pants leg and the bullet hole. He tied it, and wriggled a small stick through the knot, twisted it until the cloth bit tight into his flesh.

His only cheering thought was to blank out again. But he didn't, and just lay back and rested for a while with his head hanging down and his eyes closed. Then the shadows deepened and he roused himself, lifted his head and made whistling noises at his horse that was snatching at bunch grass.

'Stop feedin' your belly, goddamnit,'

he said in a croaky whisper. 'Come over here.' The horse lifted its head and moved in closer, and Harry made a grab for the trailing reins with his left hand.

He went over onto his side, but by pulling on the reins he got himself up to a sitting position again. The pain was excruciating, as he manoeuvred himself until the horse was standing side-on to him. Still clinging to the reins, he gripped the near stirrup and, using his weight, managed to pull the saddle back into position on the horse's back. He pulled again, made it to his right knee with the stirrup leather cutting into the front of his face. He dragged hard and reached up for the saddle horn, but it was too much and he went back to his knees.

For a long moment he stayed there, propped on one knee, cursing between short, pain-filled breaths. 'Ain't goin' to make this,' he seethed. 'Looks like you're on your own.'

He reached up and with the fingers

of his left hand, fumbled at the cinch clip until the strap fell free. He pulled until the saddle and its blanket tumbled to the ground in front of him, and he cursed again.

'Now get goin'. Go home. You got all sorts o' good feed back there.'

Uncertain of what was happening, the worried horse moved away ten feet, then twenty. Then it stopped and looked back.

'Go on. You might even get to bring me some help,' Harry called out painfully and near to despair.

The horse eventually turned away and moved off, faded into the darker shadows of the trees. Harry lay exhausted and weak. Already the chill of night was flowing down out of the upper heights. He forced himself to move again, to reach for his coat and pull it over his chest, then the saddle blanket. Gritting his teeth against the surges of pain, he lay very still and watched the stars as they emerged, tried to control his shivering.

19

It was full dark as Jack stood outside the Waittes house talking about Bonnet's likely plans and whereabouts. 'He'll have one or two things to settle, then he'll run,' he said. 'At the moment, he's probably lyin' low, girdin' himself at the Cooncan. That's where he'll be safest, behind Crespo Chance's guns.'

Olland and Crewes looked at each other then at Jack. Crewes nodded and Olland spoke for both of them. 'Yeah, we'll come with you.'

The three men walked up the steet to Bonnet's saloon. Jack pushed through the swing doors and the deputy and town marshal followed. There were a few men drinking and the gambling tables weren't yet busy.

Olland and Crewes stood either side of the doors. Jack's way was barred by Crespo Chance.

'This'll be that *next time* you told me to remember,' Jack said impassively, and before Chance had time to say anything like it.

'Yeah, an' you're gettin' the same answer,' Chance answered him back. 'He ain't here. An' *this* time, you can deal with *me*.'

Jack made a slight smile. 'Hmm, if that's the way you want it,' he said wearily. Then he squeezed his fist, and swung a ridge of knuckles, hard against Chance's jaw. The gunman's head jolted sharply, and he went sprawling backwards into a nearby table. Whiskey, glasses and cards showered across the saloon floor and Jack watched for Chance to claw at his gun. He stepped forward and ground his heel into the back of the man's hand, lifted, to kick the gun away from his trembling fingers.

At the same time, Olland roared enthusiastically, 'Leave that gun where it is.'

The bartender had grabbed a scatter-gun from beneath the bar. He'd started to turn it towards Jack, but Olland fired. A blur of shot exploded into the ceiling above Jack and Chance, and the barman slammed against the rear of the bar. Against a shattering sound, he then fell forward, his face mashing into the soggy cloth he'd been using to swab the counter top.

If any of the customers thought about making a move to support Chance and the bartender, the resounding crash of gunfire made them think again.

'Empty your belts,' Crewes yelled. 'An' put your guns on the table before you leave, which is *now*.'

The only one inclined to show fight was Chance. 'For all your sweat an' your struggle, Ridge, you still ain't got to Bonnet,' he goaded.

'Yeah, kind o' makes him the lucky one,' Jack said. With the barrel of his gun pushing hard into Chance's corded neck muscles, he forced the gunman to his feet. He prodded him across the floor of the saloon and out onto the sidewalk. 'I'm suggestin' you move on, mister,' he threatened. 'Very soon there'll be no one to work for.'

Jack called to Olland and Crewes, then pointed to Bonnet's office. 'Watch everythin,' he told them. He stood to one side of the door, out of the line of fire if Bonnet decided to put some bullets through it. He tried the knob, but the door was locked. 'Come on out, Bonnet. Everyone's dead, or gone.'

The great double-blast of Bonnet's shotgun took out the whole panelled centre-section of the door. It splintered into the back of the bar, peppering and shifting the scrunched-up body of the dead barman. Jack knew there was no other way of getting out of the building. Bonnet would have to come through his own office door.

In the dense silence that followed, Jack laughed a contemptuous goad. The split remains of the door were accordingly kicked open and Bonnet came bursting through. He was swinging up the barrels of his reloaded shotgun, but he'd got the positioning wrong. Jack was there, but kneeling in front of him.

It was Maitland Crewes who caught the blast from Bonnet's gun, falling sideways under the blow. Bonnet's eyes flashed, and Jack watched fascinated as the man steadied himself to raise the shotgun once again.

As the barrels levelled directly at him, Jack said quietly, 'Too late', and fired his .44 Colt revolver. The second shot from Bonnet's gun blasted into the floor, and Jack grunted as the pain blistered his upper legs.

As Bonnet died, his eyes rolled back, then closed, as he crumpled down onto Jack's legs. Desperately, Jack pushed the body away from the pain. His head fell back and he lay facing the ceiling. 'I think everyone *is dead now*,' he gasped, his breath, a thin and wearied gasp.

★ ★ ★

Many times in the night, Harry Ridge woke fully, the pain real and blunt, his throat burning for the need of water.

He lay there with bleak dreams, until the pink-gold of dawn broke from the mountain and lit the floor of the gully. Later, the warmth of first light touched him, and his taut muscles softened. 'Shouldn't be *too* cold when they find me,' he mused wretchedly.

For the first time he thought of his revolver. He'd lost the Winchester when he was thrown from the saddle, but the Colt was still beside him, only fallen from the holster. There were five shots in the cylinder, and he had six more in his cartridge belt. Enough to signal with, should anyone come looking for him.

But he had to wait, give whoever it was time to get near. Every movement hurt him, and blowflies had discovered a fresh, gory source of interest.

After another almost unbearable hour, he raised the gun in his left hand, braced his elbow and fired twice in rapid succession. 'That was real dumb,' he mumbled. 'One, then ten seconds, maybe more to give 'em a bearin'.' He waited for ten minutes, thinking it was closer to an hour, then he fired again.

An eternity passed, and he dragged himself into a position where his head and shoulders were propped up against the saddle and he could look along the gully. Two unused cartridges were in the gun, and he waited some more endless time before raising the gun again. He pulled on the trigger until the hammer clicked against the dead cartridges, then he cursed, and flung the empty gun out into the thick carpet of bracken and pine needles. 'Are you all blind an' deaf? I'm here,' he yelled, until his voice finally cracked and failed.

He rolled on to his belly, and, shoving with his left foot and clawing with his right hand, he struggled forward. He headed down the gully, until the blackness came for him again. Then, in insensible confusion, he rolled over until the brightness of the sun beat against his closed eyelids.

20

From his bunk in the sheriff's office, Jack grimaced, turned on his side and propped himself with an elbow. Nancy Cayne and Doc Pagham were standing close to him, talking. Nancy turned, reached for his hand and smiled.

'How'd I get *here*? I thought we were all dead,' he said.

Doc Pagham picked up his bag and looked down at Jack. 'You're a Ridge an' a sheriff. It's everyone else that dies,' he said, with a shade of irony. 'Your legs ain't too pretty, an' probably sting a bit, but that's all. Bonnet's dead though, an' so's his barman. Crewes'll be stiff for a week, but he'll live. Take more'n some bird shot to cut down a man o' that size. I've left you somethin' for the pain, when it comes on.'

Jack thought back to the gunfight in the Cooncan, the chilling movement of

Bonnet's shotgun. He gasped, shivered as Pagham left the room.

'It's been an age since we sat holdin' hands, Nancy. Must've been that time in Spanker's apple orchard,' he said after a moment.

Nancy smiled. 'I've never been anywhere near someone called Spanker's apple orchard . . . ever.'

Jack laughed. 'Oh, right,' he said. He raised himself up some more, and the soreness made him wince. 'How many bottles o' stun juice did the doc leave behind? Talkin' makes my legs hurt.'

'Then shut up.' Nancy looked hesitant. 'I'm sorry for what I said about Harry. It's difficult sometimes to control resentment, your view of things.'

'Yeah, I know it. But most everyone's paid their dues now . . . except for Tayler Gemson. I still got to take care o' that.'

'Gemson? He was shot out at one of our line shacks. You didn't know?'

'No, I didn't.' Jack's voice was

suddenly strained. 'Who was it?'

Nancy shook her head. 'Nobody seems to know. Amos found him . . . what was left. He said the buzzards must have been there a few days. There's some that's saying it was — '

'Yeah, I can guess what some are sayin', Nancy,' Jack interrupted. 'Why wasn't I told?'

'I guess *someone* would have, when you were less busy. I didn't think it would be *me*.'

Jack made to climb from the bunk. Nancy looked surprised and took a step back.

'You should be thinkin' o' leavin', Nancy, not lookin',' Jack said with a roguish grin. 'So if you don't mind, I got me places to go, an' people to see.'

'There's nothing that urgent. You need to rest up,' Nancy said, as she backed out of the room.

But Jack paid little attention. The thought of his next confrontation took the edge off his pains. At no time had he forgotten or stopped worrying about his brother, and now he needed to find out about Tayler Gemson.

'Comeback's got a paid deputy,' he called out. 'Olland can look after the town for a while.'

He managed to clamber on to a horse, and with Amos Heron he rode out to the line shack. By that time Gemson had been buried, but his saddle, gunbelt and Spencer rifle had been left for Jack to see. Jack saw that three shots had been fired from Gemson's gun, meaning that at least Gemson had returned some sort of fire, and not been backshot. Even so, to Jack's way of thinking, it wasn't quite enough to implicate Harry.

However, when Jack and Olland returned to town, Crewes met them in the middle of the street with the predictable news. 'It was Harry who shot and killed Gemson,' he reported earnestly, and before Jack had dismounted. 'Orville Grate's rode in to tell us that he saw him do it. Grate's the marshal of Eldon who was followin''

Gemson. He trailed Harry as far as he could ... took a shot ... shouted but heard nothin'. Says he coulda brought him down, Jack. You got to go up there. It's dead-or-alive now, marshal says.'

'Where? Where was this?'

'Where he shot Harry? Up near the Mossbank ... south end o' the gully.'

'Where's this goddamn good-news marshal now?'

'Don't know, but he's somewhere's about. Feisty ol' goat, said we ought to clear up our own back yard.'

'You sure his name weren't Gregor Poe?' Jack muttered. After he'd changed and rested, Jack sat for a long time on his own, thinking. Eventually he grabbed his hat and gunbelt, and left his office. Crewes saw him stuffing corn dodgers and coffee into the saddle bags of a rimrock bay he'd got from the corral. He tried to argue him out of the trip.

'You are helpin' to clean up the county, Jack. An' Miss Sophie's given all them ranchers time. She sure ain't much like her ol' man,' he said, and patted the horse on its sturdy rump. 'Why don't you get on with the job that's here, let Marshal Grate bring Harry in?'

The sheriff was exasperated with explaining. 'Because he's already shot him. Harry might be up there restin' dead, for all I know.'

Crewes knew that, but was frustrated. 'I meant, you wouldn't get *me* goin' after *my* own brother . . . if I had one.' With that, the big town marshal turned away dejectedly and trailed off down the street.

A short time later, Jack heaved himself painfully into his saddle. No one acknowledged or spoke to him as he jiggled the broad-backed bay out of town, but some who knew Gemson muttered amongst themselves.

'I wonder if that's the last we've seen of our good sheriff?' one of the older ranchers said. 'Pity the poor wretch who goes up against him, even if he is blood kin.'

'We should all be supportin' him,' another man said. 'He's the first law officer we had who ain't crooked or gone that way. An' his brother Harry weren't guilty of anythin' before all this started, so why'd he start now? But you're right about one thing, though: I wouldn't want to be between 'em when the shootin' starts.'

★ ★ ★

Jack crossed the northern half of Raising Cayne, then he swung south-west for a climbing trail to the Ozarks. He knew close enough where the old Eldon marshal, Orville Grate, must have fired upon Harry, that someone in trouble could find stuff to feed themselves. There was plenty of berries and wild onions, rabbit and bird for trapping, fresh water in the gullies.

21

Jack couldn't think of a lot to say, right off. 'Harry. How long you been here like this, Harry?' he asked, after quickly making a check of the surrounding area.

Harry struggled as Jack's words penetrated his brain. He swam up and out of the dark, into bright, glowing sunlight. Blurred, but directly above him he made out the worried and sweat-stained face of his brother. 'About four, maybe five years . . . nothin' to eat or drink either . . . don't feel too good,' he laboured with his answer.

'Yeah, you look like it. Most of *us* would've died long ago,' Jack said.

'An' *you* want help . . . I knew you'd come. Get me back on a horse . . . point me in the right direction.'.

'You always were the toughest, Harry.

But right now, you really ain't. I got us some food an' some coffee. We'll rest up a while an' exchange swingin' lead stories . . . who's been shootin' who, an' why. You're still in deep trouble.'

'Yeah? What's in your pie box?'

An hour later, after half-a-dozen corn dodgers each that had been soaked in hot coffee laced with laudanum, the Ridge brothers weren't feeling too bad. They told each other of what had happened in the last few days.

'I let Gemson fire three times before I shot him, Jack,' Harry said. '*He* had his chances, Pa didn't.'

'I know, an' I believe you, Harry. An' there's no reason why you can't come back with me. At least now, you'll get a fair trial. We've done what we set out to do.'

'Maybe,' Harry answered.

'Where's your horse?'

'Huh, who knows. The old whey-belly's probably eatin' its way back to Sunbird.'

'I guessed as much,' Jack said. 'So I

brought us a big-ended mare. We can double up. Do you reckon you can make it back?'

Harry gave a small, yielding smile. 'Maybe, if I ride in front. Do you remember Pa once tellin' us that when some folk get ill, they go to sleep until they get well? It's lettin' the body heal itself, or somethin' like that.'

'It was about sick sheep, as I recall,' Jack said.

'Well, whoever it was, them three days an' nights have worked for me. I ain't felt so good since before I went to ground. But I still got more goddamn holes than I started out with.'

'Once I got you tucked up in jail, I'll get Doc Pagham to clean you up. As you're my brother, maybe even before. Here,' Jack said, handing Harry the .44 revolver that matched his own. 'I've reloaded it for you. Now you can shoot me, if you change your mind.'

'I can't do that Jack, not from where I'm ridin'. Besides, we'll need both our guns if we run into any o' Gemson's friends, or that ol' Marshal Grate.'

'Yeah, an' it sure would look odd, bringin' in a trigger-itch outlaw who's still wearin his guns. If we reach town safely, maybe I'll think o' snappin' you with some cuffs ... tie you up or somethin'.'

★   ★   ★

The day's heat had changed to the chill of sunset when the sheriff and his prisoner jostled into Comeback. They stopped outside the jail and climbed awkwardly from the sturdy built rim-rocker. The town marshal who had been dozing in his chair jumped to his feet as Jack kicked the door shut. He made a wild grab for his gun, but Jack held up his hands.

'Whoa, feller. Take it easy. It's *us*, Jack an' Harry,' he said.

Crewes was staggered at the sight of the brothers who were gaunt and weary. Their stubbled faces were caked with trail dust, their clothes grimed and smeared with blood.

Harry laughed. 'It ain't been a clambake, Maitland, an' I'm genuinely pleased to be back. I once spent a night in the cooler at West Point,' he said, eyeing the bars of a cell. 'It was clean . . . very clean, but lacked the friendly charm o' this here lodgin'.'

Crewes smiled uncomfortably and looked at Jack. 'So, which of these cells shall I put him in?' he asked.

'The one with drapes an' carpets,' Jack responded sharply.

'Carpets? One of 'em ain't hardly got a floor.'

'Then put him in the other one, for Chris'sakes,' Jack growled edgily.

Harry nudged Crewes as they walked through the steel-strapped cell door. 'Don't know who's salted his tail. Do you reckon he's nervous o' somethin'?'

Crewes still looked ill at ease. 'Yeah, I do. It's goin' to take more'n Marshal Grate to keep a Bonnet an' Gemson mob down. *If* he ever shows here again. Maybe he's rode right back to Eldon.'

'Have you seen a mob?' Harry asked.

'There's some been blusterin' on the street . . . tellin' anyone in earshot that the town's givin' itself a string party.'

Crewes stepped back into the front office. Jack was sitting at his desk with his head down, buried in the fold of his arms. The town marshal put his great meaty hand on Jack's shoulder. 'You got yourself an extra gun,' he said, with such ingenuousness that Jack nearly laughed.

'Thanks, Mait,' Jack said looking up. 'Can you order up some food from the hotel? An' get Doc Pagham to bring some physic over here, pronto. If you see Grate, tell him the outlaw's caught an' landed in jail.'

Outside in the street, men gathered in little groups to suggest odds on the unavoidable showdown between the Bonnet and Ridge factions. Others left town on furtive assignations. Others simply left town. Crespo Chance hadn't heeded Jack's warning, even now, was operating from the saloon. It was he who'd helped inflame the situation with luridly exaggerations of Harry's ruthless shooting of Tayler Gemson.

Chance was a hired gunman, but he was also an exploiter of situations. He notioned running the Cooncan, even creating his own partnership with the town's alliance, but, pending a decision on Gabriel Bonnet's estate, Jack had already elected to shut down the saloon.

Doc Pagham attended to Harry's wounds. Fortunately there were no bullets to remove. The injuries made by Orville Grate's rifle were deep-fleshed and painful though, needed washing, wadding with salve and clean dressing.

Pagham picked up on the intending gunfight and was pleased to get away. 'I'll set up a field hospital outside o' town. Maybe I'll see you all there,' he said cynically, 'if you're *lucky*,' he added on leaving.

When two plattered dinners were brought over from the hotel, Jack unlocked the cell and Harry emerged to sit with him at the desk in the front office. As they ate, the brothers discussed the possibility of making a stand at the jail. Just after they'd finished, Crick Olland arrived. He had Orville Grate with him, and Harry greeted the marshal without showing any ill feeling.

'It's safer in *here* than just about anywhere out there, if you get my meanin', Marshal,' he said.

'Yeah, even for those who ain't chose sides,' Grate replied, then turned to Jack. 'I thought if I got scarce for long enough, you'd bring him in yourself. Looks like I weren't wrong.' Grate winced at the aching in his legs as he eased himself into a spoke-back chair. 'When this little jamboree's done, I'm retirin',' he growled. The Eldon marshal's attention then went back to Harry. 'Now, Harry Ridge, suppose you tell me exactly what happened up at that line shack. If it helps some, I don't reckon me an' Tayler Gemson would ever o' been a close workin' relationship.'

Harry described all that had happened, or all that he could remember happening. Of the actual shooting, Grate's manner was decidedly less scratchy. He looked considerately at Harry's wounds. 'From what *I* saw, my action was justified,' he said, 'but now on hearin' your side, it proves that seein' ain't necessarily the whole truth.'

'Ain't *that* a fact,' Harry agreed with some relief.

'O' course there's got to be a little doubt ... stands to reason,' Grate chided gently. Then the marshal was back to Jack again. 'This is your extravaganza, Sheriff Ridge. But I'd like to know what you're expectin' an' *when*. I didn't mean for that retirement o' mine to start from the toes pointin' to daisies position.'

'Well, they know we're back. If they drink enough, they'll be barkin' at the moon. *That's* our edge, an' *that's* when they'll come.'

Crewes went into the small stock-room. 'This afternoon I did the rounds . . . requisitioned most o' the ammo in town. That was my smart idea for the year,' he called out. 'We've got us plenty rifles an' handguns, so we can give a good account of ourselves if we have to. Remember it ain't the size of the ol' dog in the fight, but the size of the fight in the ol' dog.'

Jack and Harry exchanged an amused, wry look, and Crick Olland said he'd walk the street. 'They won't have drunk the Cooncan dry yet, but if any of 'em do start makin' their way over, you can let me in the back door,' he suggested.

Jack nodded and Olland left the jail. Crewes looked accusingly at Grate. 'If you'd stayed in your own field, all this might have turned out a bit different.'

Grate shook his head resignedly. 'Maybe. But you wouldn't have slept any sounder on it, believe me.'

It was silent and tense for a minute or so, then Jack said, 'Perhaps it's my fault for bringin' you back, Harry. But there's still a way out if you want to take it, if you go *now*.' Jack looked from his brother to Grate for a response.

The marshal nodded his head in agreement. 'As far as the law's concerned, you're cleared of any wrong doin', so I've got no argument. Fact bein', an' truth be told, if you was to make enough noise on clearin' town, you could draw 'em away from *here*. One life for three?'

'Yeah, *mine*, an' that ain't what — ' Harry started on an offended protest, but Grate interrupted him.

'Now, ain't *that* a fact,' he said, and broke a smile for the first time.

22

Harry knew that in their situation, it was difficult for any sworn-in lawman to make a decision about what he should or shouldn't do. They were going on personal feeling and fairness as opposed to legal hair-splitting. But it did leave him with an alternative about where to die.

'Well, thanks for your collective advice, gentlemen,' Harry said. 'I'm of the opinion it don't amount to a hill o' beans, but *mostly*, it's the outlaw life that ain't for me. Especially the bit where you get your neck stretched under a cottonwood. So I'm stayin' right here,' he decided.

'Ahh, good,' Jack said. 'We're gettin' to die together, like a proper family. Have your Colt back, Harry, an' grab a rifle. Mait, stack those cartridges in the corner . . . pile somethin' round 'em.

Watch the rear door for Crick. I'll cover the front with Harry. Orville, if you don't mind, take up the side window.'

Harry looked around him at the unsure faces. 'Hey, Jack,' he said. 'What's that promotion they give you on the battlefield? The one where you don't get any extra pay, 'cause they don't think you'll live long enough to collect it?'

'Brevet.'

'Yeah, Brevet. Well, you just got it, Brother.'

Jack grinned and turned to look through the dust-coated window into the street. 'Should've got these cleaned,' he muttered.

The quartet of defenders took up their positions. Jack and the marshal carried Winchesters, and they had laid scatterguns at their feet as well as filled gunbelts.

A menacing silence filled the street, but now and again they caught the drifting strains of drunk courage from the Cooncan. Crewes pushed the big desk up against the front door and they continued their wait.

After fifteen minutes a group of men rode at full tilt past the jail, and they all levered shells into the chambers of their rifles.

'Looks like Chance has stopped plyin' his friends with booze,' Harry observed.

'What do you mean?' Jack asked.

'He's ridin' out front. An' Amos Heron's with 'em.'

Jack squinted into the street. 'Ungrateful son-of-a-bitch. When Harvey got killed, Crick should've laid him out here, instead o' Doc Pagham's.'

Shortly, the unmistakable sound of boots and spurs announced the arrival of someone on the puncheoned sidewalk. They rapped sharply on the rear door of the jail.

'That's Crick. Now we really are a handful,' Crewes said, as he let the deputy sheriff in.

Olland looked around the inside of the jail and hastily pulled another rifle from the gun rack. 'Shouldn't be long now,' he said, thumbing shells into the magazine. 'Remarkable what a gallon o' that Cooncan bear piss does for your confidence.'

The world outside turned quiet, presaged Grate's whispered words, 'Here they come, boys.' Then he eased up the window and pushed the barrel of his rifle across the sill.

The shouting and bravado increased and the mob spilled from the sidewalk to fan out across the street directly in front of the jail. One man who appeared more in control than the rest, placed a foot on the low wooden step and pulled the brim of his hat further down on his forehead.

Jack turned away from the other window. 'Who the hell's that?'

Without looking, Olland answered. 'Aubert Rhimes, the ramrod o' Hangin' Gate.'

'So, that's his name. Well, Mr Rhimes don't look as well dressed today, does he?'

Rhimes was wearing working overalls, not his customary hickory suit. He was the man whom Onslow Stern had given a good beating out at Sunbird.

'They really shouldn't bunch up like that,' Harry said turning to his brother. 'OK if we were gettin' a herd together, but *out here, under our guns?*'

'Maybe it's what we want 'em to do, Harry,' Jack suggested.

Olland was peering through the side window, over Orville Grate's shoulder. 'I can see Chance is holdin' back. He ain't gamblin' with *his* hide, eh, Harry?'

Jack had a quick look across the street. 'No, he ain't,' he said. 'An' he don't take advice either.' He rolled away from the window with his back against the wall. 'Rhimes is comin' up.'

The butt of a gun banged loudly against the door and Rhimes's voice called out. 'We come for Harry Ridge. Send him out an' there'll be no trouble.'

'You don't need no goddamn clown's outfit to make you a funny man, do you, mister?' Jack yelled back instantly. 'Now, get away from that door, or you'll be travellin' halfway across the street on it.'

Jack beckoned to Crewes. 'Shove the desk aside. An' if you think what Rhimes had to offer was amusin', just watch this. I'll be back shortly,' he said. Crewes eased the desk away from the door and Jack pulled the door open enough for him to step out onto the sidewalk. He faced up to Rhimes who'd immediately taken a step back into the street. The ramrod's Colt was gripped tight in his hand. But Jack knew it was the tightness of apprehension, that Rhimes wasn't up for any immediate gunfighting.

Shuffling uneasily behind the Hanging Gate man were a few of the Gemson crowd, and Jack lifted his rifle towards them. 'There's a prisoner I got to protect, an' you all know why. But he's my brother, an' that makes me more easy on the trigger. Same for them holed up in the jail. All you men, just think about it.'

As Jack spoke, he remembered Sophie saying that she hated Comeback, and what he'd said to Radford Cayne about good territory, only bad people.

'Huh. The futile noise of a cornered rat,' Rhimes sneered.

An' them's the rats that'll bite you, Jack thought, but didn't say it.

Rhimes waved his Colt and turned to face the men backing him. 'We goin' to let him talk us out o' gettin' to the killer? Let's take him.'

Jack was swearing at his blunder, the fatal mistake of getting the situation wrong, when, from somewhere at the rear of the shifting mob, a gun blasted off. He felt a stinging thump across the side of his neck and swore again, ducked as the blast of two scatterguns crashed out from behind him. He spun back to the crowd and levered off two bullets as he backed up the steps to the door of the jail.

'That'll be them rats,' he yelled.

Up against the jail's front door, he sent off another two rounds low into the front of the mob. A man faltered with a cry of furious pain, and Jack saw him collapse with both legs smashed and bloodied across the knees. Then there was a yell from Harry and he was dragged back into the jail, someone slammed the door shut behind them.

'I'll wager *that* upset 'em,' Harry said, as Jack crouched on the floor, gulping in air. A moment later, a deafening hail of bullets splintered the clapboarding and smashed in the windows that fronted the jailhouse.

23

'You bastards. I was goin' to clean them,' Jack yelled. He kicked out at the shards of wood and glass as he pushed his back against the inside front wall.

Only the rear half of the jail that contained the cells was laid to brick. No one had ever considered there'd be such a ferocious and deadly barrage against its prisoners. In a matter of seconds, the cells resonated madly with the buzz and ping of ricocheting bullets. But in the street, there were a number of men flattening the dust. They were mostly wounded, but some went for shelter, while others continued to smother the jail with blanket gunfire.

Orville Grate and Harry sat crouched behind the desk. Crick Olland stood rigid in back of the stockroom and Crewes was crazily counting the bullets. Harry rolled onto all fours and looked across at his brother.

'Caught the head of a big blue norther once up in Nebraska. This ain't much compared,' he shouted.

Marshal Grate joined in. 'You'll never grow old in this job, Sheriff.'

'I already did,' Jack yelled back.

As the mighty broadside faltered, Grate eyed the shattered room. 'Well, now it's our turn. Let's not get crazy or angry. Stay in control, an' give 'em hell.'

The guardians of the jail discharged a fast and lethal stream of fire from its windows. They were heavily outnumbered, but they were more precise and expert. Straightaway Jack took out Crespo Chance with a purposeful shot. The make-believe saloon keeper had targeted himself against a big sash window, and when Jack's bullet struck him he spun around. He steadied to front them across the smoky street, then staggered before going to his knees. He looked up and, as he died, both hands gripped his Colt like the throat of an adversary.

In front of Chance, already with face glued to the street dirt, was a man shot by Orville Grate. To the side, another body was sprawled awkwardly, but still alive and moaning for help. Harry had accounted for at least two more. They weren't dead yet, but soon one of them would be. Amos Heron was hanging from the building's low eaves. He'd been on the roof, caught a bullet from Olland's rifle and rolled until he snagged on the overhanging tie-beam. Enfolding a water butt, the Hanging Gate ramrod known as Aubert Rhimes, twitched convulsively, his toes thumping the barrel in disappointment as life failed him.

'Stop firin',' Grate yelled, and the men in the jail turned away from the windows. They sank to the floor and looked at each other, stunned. The onslaught had been desperate but the sudden quiet was almost as fearful. It filled the jail, merged with the pungent bite of gunpowder. None of

the men had their eye on the rear
door of the jail, and none of them
caught the movement as it crashed
open. There was a loud, hollow bang,
and Jack let out a grunt of pain. 'Not
again,' he yelled and instinctively
doubled up. But before Harry had
reached him, he was stretching his
legs out and pumping another round
into his Winchester.

'Where you hit, Jack?' Harry asked
him anxiously.

'Ah, somewhere not vital. But I tell
you this, Harry: there's now so many
bits an' pieces of us Ridges lyin' about
the territory, I reckon one o' my fine
surgeon colleagues could build us
another brother.'

Harry laughed nervously, then looked
across at where the marshal was sitting
under the shattered remains of the
window. 'Are you still kickin', Orville?'
he wanted to know.

The marshal had dragged himself up
into the spoke-back chair but there was
no response from him.

'Oh Christ, Jack, they got Orville,' Harry shouted.

Jack mumbled something obscure about all things being equal. His head started to dip, and blood swelled around the top of his gunbelt.

Harry cursed. He stood up quickly and stepped towards the front door.

'Where you goin'?' Olland shouted, his voice cracked with alarm.

Harry looked back steadily as he took the door handle. 'I don't know how many out there's fit to fight on, Crick, but there's two dyin' in here, an' one of 'em's my brother. There's no need to make it any more.'

Jack was beyond making any real movement, and before Olland or Crewes could try and stop him, Harry pulled the door open. 'Try an' get me then,' he yelled, his voice lost in the instant crash of answering gunfire.

Jack groaned softly and crumpled further to the floor. Holding their Winchesters, Olland and Crewes moved out onto the sidewalk. From either side of the doorway, they watched Harry running towards the corral. It was full dark now and bright flashes were flaring from his .44 Colt revolver. Bullets chewed into the dust around his feet and whirred around his head like fat sawflies.

As Olland and Crewes pumped bullets into the dimly lit mob, they heard a strangled yell. As the group of men turned back towards the jail, they were caught between a town marshal, a deputy sheriff and Harry Ridge. They scattered, hurling themselves frantically into whatever cover they found along the raised sidewalks.

Harry had pulled a horse from the corral and doubled back. Hatless, and fair hair flying, he plunged through the mob at a gallop. He was bent low over the horse's neck, and swung to the ground in front of the jail. He ran, leaped to the jailhouse steps and gently pressed the barrel of his gun into the flesh of Crick Olland's nose. 'Don't let my brother die,' he said icily.

'Hell, Mait, I thought he was goin' to shoot me,' Olland said a moment later, as Harry waved back at the troubled pair.

Crewes looked thoughtfully at the deputy. 'If Jack does die, he'll come back, an' he will,' he said. 'You'd best get Doc Pagham. He won't be too far off.'

★ ★ ★

Crewes brought an unbroken lamp from the cells, and under its light, the doc made a swift check and tidy job on Jack and Orville Grate. They were then carried to the hotel, and for what remained of the night, a relative calm settled over Comeback.

By mid morning, the remains of bloodshed had been mostly removed from the street. Marshal Grate was into his mending, and Jack was weak, but comfortable. As they lay in adjacent cots, the marshal turned stiffly to Jack. 'How long you goin' to be laid up?' he asked.

'The doc says I been shot at an' hit more times than's reasonable. He's recommended nursin' for a couple o' years at least.'

Grate made an effortless laugh. 'Supposin' the town's happy with your work, how's it goin' to get along without you?'

'That's up to them. You're askin' a damn fine load o' questions, Orville?'

Grate squeezed his eyes tight shut, more with deliberation than pain. 'I was just wonderin', more thinkin' about me, givin' up the law work.'

'So, there's an alternative?'

'Yeah, sort of. While you were roundin' up your brother, I had a look around. There'a lot o' business got freed up recently, an' I got to thinkin' about saloon keepin'. Then I considered bankin'. But I reckon I've settled on men's furnishin's, with an annexe for a wash an' brush up, hair cut, shave an' beard trim. An' if my ol' eyes ain't been deceived, it'll be regular money. This godforsaken, flea-bit town could sure do with *somethin'* to clean it up. I'll have me a grand openin',' he was saying, as Nancy Cayne stepped quietly into the room.

Nancy looked relieved at Grate, then sat next to Jack's bed. 'I'm sorry about what happened . . . the mess you're all in,' she said, the sincerity natural and plain to see. 'And for sitting next to your bed, watching your pain . . . not being able to do much.'

Jack was about to agree when, the door opened and Doc Pagham came in. he too glanced at Grate then Nancy. 'Perhaps one day you can visit him when he's somewhere other than a sick bed,' he said. Then he looked at Jack. 'I think you've got yourself another visitor.'

Someone tapped hesitantly on the door, and everyone in the room exchanged questioning glances.

'I hope it ain't someone with a gun,' Grate rumbled. 'My retirement's almost started.'

But it was Harry who came bustling

in, his eyes drifting around the room.

Jack was surprised and unprepared. 'Harry, I was just thinkin' about you,' he said.

Harry grinned. 'I'm sure he don't mean that, ma'am,' he said to Nancy while pulling his hat from his head. 'Max knew where I'd be. He came to tell me that you were all right, an' that Justice Durram says there ain't too much to be troubled by. He says they're more likely to bury the warrant than me.' Harry looked towards Orville Grate for added confirmation.

'The sod's already turned, son,' the marshal said, and winked his approval.

Jack was staring wearily at his brother when Seth Carlisle slipped discreetly through the open door. He smiled at Nancy, nodded at Jack and spoke to Harry. 'The old stream bed's fillin' up,' he said. 'Be holdin' finger trout by the time it flows down to Sunbird. You ain't bossin' a salt flat after all.'

'How do you know, Seth? You been sittin' out, while we been gun stompin' with the locals?' Jack asked with a roguish grin.

'I ain't been sittin' out, or in, or anywhere. There's still a ranch to be run, even with no water, in case you boys forgot,' Seth replied in equal good humour. 'It was a group o' ranchers an' Deputy Olland. They rode up to the timberline where the barrier was ... went to have a looksee for 'emselves. The high peak rains have run a second watercourse ... forced an easier route down to the *old* stream bed.' He looked back at Jack. 'Now there's nothin' to raise a fight over. I reckon it's finished.'

Jack was unbelievably tired. 'The big bad beasts are dead an' gone, Seth, an' them that figured on replacin' 'em. *But nothin's ever finished,*' he said wearily. 'Things just quieten down for a while. I think it must be one o' the reasons we have armies.' With that thought in mind, Jack made up his mind to return to the West Point academy. Comeback had itself another sheriff in Crick

Olland, and Nancy Cayne and Sophie Waittes could start sewing the quilts.

Harry had already guessed his brother's campaign, his hopes and fears. 'I'm listenin' to Seth, agreein' with him too,' he said. 'The ranch is in my name, so I'd best start runnin' it. An' don't you get too daring,' he said looking keenly at Jack. 'You told me most generals die in bed.'

THE END

We do hope that you have enjoyed reading this large print book.

Did you know that all of our titles are available for purchase?

We publish a wide range of high quality large print books including:
**Romances, Mysteries, Classics General Fiction
Non Fiction and Westerns**

Special interest titles available in large print are:
**The Little Oxford Dictionary
Music Book, Song Book
Hymn Book, Service Book**

Also available from us courtesy of Oxford University Press:
**Young Readers' Dictionary
(large print edition)
Young Readers' Thesaurus
(large print edition)**

For further information or a free brochure, please contact us at:
**Ulverscroft Large Print Books Ltd.,
The Green, Bradgate Road, Anstey,
Leicester, LE7 7FU, England.
Tel:** (00 44) **0116 236 4325
Fax:** (00 44) **0116 234 0205**

Other titles in the
Linford Western Library:

DESTINATION BOOT HILL

Peter Mallett

Wayne Coulter rode with a gang until an ambush left him wounded, and he might have died if it hadn't been for Henry Mallen and his granddaughter Julie. However, Mallen and Julie are also in trouble, and when Mallen is shot dead, Coulter takes on Julie's enemies. But when a former gang member betrays the outlaws for reward money — it means death. Gun smoke and hot lead will rage in a lethal storm to the very end . . .

TROUBLE AT TAOS

Jackson Davis

Seth Tobin rescued Ruth Simms from Crow attack, thinking that when they reached Fort Union she would be safe living with her Uncle. But as Seth heads for the Rockies, the trader Almedo and the notorious bandit leader Espinosa lust after Ruth. Soon the body count rises as the sound of guns reverberates through the mountains. Can Seth, and the wily old mountain man Dick McGhee, save Ruth from an awful fate — and reap some gold by way of reward . . . ?

SATAN'S GUN

Bill Williams

Nineteen-year-old Sam Bryson faces a conflict that will test his courage, character and faith. Raised mostly by his grandparents, Sam was made to practise with his pistol every day, except Sunday. Yet Albert Bryson's beloved wife had raised Sam to reject violence. Bryson orders Sam and his cousin, Jack, to hunt down his ranch hand's murderer, Sharkey Kelsall. Sam Bryson has no desire to kill, but soon discovers that when his own life is threatened he must protect himself.

BLUECOAT RENEGADE

Dale Graham

Lieutenant Chadwick Stanton is based at Fort Leavenworth in Kansas. His over-extravagant life-style causes him to initiate a robbery of the regimental payroll, but blame is placed squarely on his envied and hated rival, fellow officer, Captain Bentley Wallace. The trial, a foregone conclusion, results in the shamed officer being drummed out of the service. Now Ben wants retribution. But Stanton, in a cataclysmic showdown in a remote Wyoming canyon, is determined to thwart him. Can Ben find justice?

HARD MEN RIDING

Elliot Conway

Texan man Raynor, and his Mexican compadre Santos, had once been in Jake Petch's gang of bank robbers. After a raid in Grantsburg, Petch had bushwhacked Raynor and Santos, left them for dead and taken all the gold. Two years later, Raynor learns that Petch is now a big rancher in Arizona, and sets out with Santos on the vengeance trail. They leave a long tally of dead men before they finally face Petch. Can they settle the score?

JUST CALL ME CLINT

Chad Hammer

'Just call me Clint,' he told the town the day he rode in and Wolflock would never be the same again. To some he looked like a drifter, whilst others were sure he spelt trouble. Whatever he was, Clint was different to anyone they'd seen before. Here was a man with a past who'd come to their town to avenge a great wrong. Clint would either succeed, or go down shooting. He was that breed of man.